Touch and Go

by

EJ Towler

Touch and Go

Cover Art by *Kristian Norris*

The Wild Rose Press, Inc.
PO Box 708
Adams Basin, NY 14410-0708
Visit us at www.thewildrosepress.com

Publishing History
First Edition, 2023
Trade Paperback ISBN 978-1-5092-4762-2
Digital ISBN 978-1-5092-4763-9

Published in the United States of America

The word divorce froze Air Force Lieutenant Colonel Jennifer Ryan's heart. Despite the internal battle she stood, spine pencil straight, and recited her mental mantra, don't give in to the hurt and anger. Nothing will be gained by crying or losing your temper. Their daughters deserved a stable home. The constant military moves were disruptive enough. No matter what she had to endure their daughters came first and they loved their father, unconditionally.

For balance she placed her fingertips on the kitchen counter, drew in a long, slow breath, let it out gently. "What part of 'I don't want a divorce' are you having trouble comprehending?" Her voice was low, but intense as she spoke over her shoulder to her husband.

Stalling to face him, she poured coffee into her brightly painted dachshund mug. The cup warmed her fingers. The aroma of dark roast coffee calmed her. She'd seen the signs, another affair, denied it. Damn! She was one of those women with her head in the sand. Emotions rose in her throat like bile.

Phillip paced the kitchen, turned to face her. "Whether you believe it or not our marriage is finished. I want a divorce." He leaned in, his eyes cold, hostile, the stare so intense it caused her to hold her breath.

His harsh demeanor and tone chilled her to the bone. "I can't accept it is. You've had affairs before and came back." She unconsciously rubbed the top of the 1950s rectangle table. The first piece of furniture they'd scrimped and saved to buy.

Praise for EJ Towler

EJ Towler first book, *Stealth Maneuvers*, has multiple 5 star reviews on Amazon.

One Little Lie, a psychological thriller, was released January 2023. This book finished second in Finish the Damn Book Contest by Chesapeake Romance Writers.

Touch and Go won second place in the Fall In Love New England Reader's Choice Contest.

Dedication

This book is dedicated to my sister Linda: my travel companion, biggest supporter, and best friend. I love you but we will never agree on the silverware arrangement in the dishwasher.

Chapter One

The word divorce froze Air Force Lieutenant Colonel Jennifer Ryan's heart. Despite the internal battle, she stood, spine pencil straight, and recited her mental mantra, *Don't give in to the hurt and anger. Nothing will be gained by crying or losing your temper.* Their daughters deserved a stable home. The constant military moves were disruptive enough. No matter what she had to endure, their daughters came first, and they loved their father unconditionally.

For balance, she placed her fingertips on the kitchen counter, drew in a long, slow breath, let it out gently. "What part of 'I don't want a divorce' are you having trouble comprehending?" Her voice was low, but intense as she spoke over her shoulder to her husband.

Stalling to face him, she poured coffee into her brightly painted dachshund mug. The cup warmed her fingers, and the aroma of dark roast coffee calmed her. She'd seen the signs, another affair, denied it. Damn! She was one of *those* women with her head in the sand. Emotions rose in her throat like bile.

Phillip paced the kitchen, turned to face her. "Whether you believe it or not, our marriage is finished. I want a divorce." He leaned in, his eyes cold, hostile, the stare so intense it caused her to hold her breath.

His harsh demeanor and tone chilled her to the bone. "I can't accept it is. You've had affairs before and came

1

back." She unconsciously rubbed the top of the 1950s rectangle table. The first piece of furniture they'd scrimped and saved to buy. So many life events and decisions occurred around its polished royal blue surface. This was where they'd decided she'd return to school for her Ph.D. in clinical psychology. Sitting here, she'd shared they were having twins and had timed her contractions.

Phillip's intimidating tone hit Jennifer like pellets of hate. "I'm telling you it is over; I want a divorce. Just accept it." He shoved the chair into the table and glared. He was so close the smell of his new aftershave wafted over her.

Jennifer bit the edge of her tongue to stop the emotions and regain some semblance of composure. She raised her chin and spoke with a forced steadiness. "I gather it's another woman, *again*? Last time you demanded a divorce, you were in the midst of a hot, torrid love affair." When their gaze met, he looked away.

Her husband's dark brown hair was graying around the temples, and his sea-green eyes looked tired. The tailored Air Force uniform accented his broad shoulders and trim waist. Even after all his indiscretions, the man still set her heart a-flutter. *Damn him.*

"It's *over*." He accented the words by slamming his mug on the table. Drops of the dark liquid littered the sparking blue surface.

"If it's something else, tell me." Thanks to the private investigator, she didn't need him to answer, but she wasn't going to make this easy on him. She stood, walked past, and down the hall to retrieve her jacket. With each step, she packed away the raw feelings. He'd not see her cry, not now, not ever again.

Phillip was staring out the living room picture window when she returned. She reached up and placed her hand on his shoulder.

Jennifer knew it was reflex when he covered her hand with his. She followed his gaze to the front yard. Fall had come to Hampton Roads, Virginia. Autumn flowers were in full bloom. The pink, blue, purple, and white asters swayed as the breeze caressed them. Fat robins hunted around the toad lilies for worms surfacing from last night's rain.

They'd designed and planted the flower beds as a family. *It was such a happy time, at least for her. Now it's no more than a reminder of things lost.*

She struggled to bring her voice above a whisper. "Have you decided what's so important you'd throw away twenty years of marriage? Tell me." She needed to hear him say the words, even though they'd break her heart.

She knew all too well, Phillip's current sweet thing, Lisa Wallingford was pregnant. He'd probably knocked her up on purpose to get his hands on her multi-million-dollar trust fund. Her stomach churned with disgust. *How could she still care for this man? Why should she want him?*

"Nothing, I just want a divorce." His tone was patient but bordered on defeat. The rage had vanished; his brow seemed permanently creased.

Jennifer stepped to face him, placed a hand on his chest, and fought to ignore the remoteness in his eyes. Her voice was almost a murmur, "You know it will be like before. You'll tire of seeing the girls only on weekends and want to come home."

The fierce anger returned to his eyes and voice. "No.

3

This is different." Each word was laced with hostility. He shook his head and closed his eyes.

"What? You suddenly don't love me anymore?" she asked in cold sarcasm. Her stomach churned. She wanted to throw up all over his high-polished military shoes.

He shrugged and paused before he answered. "I love you, but not the way I should. We've grown apart; I'm not happy; you deserve better, pick one."

She should've laughed, his responses were so cliché, but instead, her question had a huge dose of sarcasm. "I gather since we made love twice last night you still find me attractive. That isn't the issue, then?"

"No." He closed his eyes and dropped his head into his left palm.

Jennifer's composure regained, she was ready to play his game. She stepped to Phillip and let her southern accent roll out with her words. "Then last night was—how shall I put this politely, a roll in the hay?" Jennifer tapped her cheek with her ring finger before continuing. "Or better yet, a pity-fuck for old time's sake?" She accented her comment with a half chuckle.

Their eyes met again. "Yes. That's all it was." Phillip's face softened for a second as he stroked her cheek with his fingertips. As quickly, the anger returned. "You're twisting what I'm saying. Stop that psychological analysis crap."

"I'm doing no such thing. So, you don't love me but still want me?" Jennifer said quickly.

"Get mad, throw something, act like any other woman would. You sound like you're ordering a pizza, not discussing a divorce. Why won't you just let me go?" Phillip threw his hands up and brushed past her.

Jennifer smiled and held up her palms. "Our

daughters don't deserve to grow up in a broken home, being passed back and forth. You forget I've been there. The answer is no, I won't agree to a divorce." The momentary wall she'd built began to cave to the oncoming emotional avalanche. Her logical thought pattern was dissolving. She broke eye contact and moved toward the table.

"Damnation, Jennifer!" He leaned on the sofa back. A muscle twitched in his jaw.

Because her hands shook, she used both to lift the cup. The motion was more for something to do than drink. She took a deep breath and asked, "Does this have anything to do with my promotion? Working in the medical field, we knew there was a chance I'd make rank quicker." She followed his gaze to the silver oak leaves on her shoulders.

"Shit, this has nothing to do with you out-ranking me." Phillip shoved his hands in his pockets and paced.

Jennifer looked at her watch. "I've got to go. I'll be late. Remember today is early release, and you need to pick up the girls. Dance is at three thirty. I'll be home by six. Dinner is in the slow cooker." She rinsed her cup and placed it in the drainer.

"I'll pick up the girls, but I won't be here for dinner," Phillip's frustration came through loud and clear as he turned and headed toward the hallway.

"Suit yourself." Jennifer shrugged and slipped into her uniform jacket. She made it to the car before she felt the sting of tears on her cheeks. At least she had the forethought to skip the mascara. As she backed the SUV from the garage, the cold reality her husband was probably already on the phone with Lisa hit her like a rogue ocean wave.

She stopped at the end of the drive and rested her head on the steering wheel. *The situation is what it is. I'm not going down without a fight. This will end my way. The question is, what way is that?*

****

Jennifer made mental notes as members of the PTSD support group shared both good and bad experiences from the past week. She knew them all and their stories. Many had faced similar situations yet reacted vastly differently to the traumas they'd suffered. So was the conundrum of the human mind.

She currently had three support groups on her case load. This was by far her favorite, though she'd never say that out loud. If there was a weakness in her practice, it was the line between counselor and client often blurred. When a client disappeared from therapy, Jennifer wondered what more she could've done. She couldn't allow herself to think about those who'd taken their lives; that was a rabbit hole to disaster.

Jennifer pulled herself from the fog and looked around the space. A year ago, the meeting room had been drab and unwelcoming. But her men, they might not be under her command, but they were under her care, which she considered a higher duty. They'd scraped the peeling gray paint and transformed the space with a coat of bright sky-blue. Someone had painted clouds on one wall, then birds soaring across the sky seemed to appear overnight: everyone proving their talent and healing in the process.

Jennifer supplied a dozen potted plants; someone else watered and tended them. They worked as a family in this space. Together, they'd created a safe haven. She knew all too well, for many, this was the only safe place they had.

Jennifer checked her watch. "Let's take a break. Grab a cup of coffee, smoke 'em if you got 'em, be back in fifteen. I brought blueberry muffins, help yourself," Jennifer announced.

As the group dispersed, she walked to the snack table and picked up a cup. "Troy," she acknowledged with a smile.

"Doc." He nodded.

Jennifer chose her words carefully; she'd seen the distress creep in over the last couple of weeks. Today the circles around his eyes were deep and dark. "You've been pretty quiet recently."

"Yep." Troy shrugged his shoulders and looked away.

She filled the mug with coffee and turned to face him. "We can sit and talk if you like." She motioned toward the metal folding chairs near the window.

He rolled the white Styrofoam between his fingers. "Not sure I'm ready."

"Okay, you sit, I'll talk." She walked to the chairs.

"That works," Troy murmured.

She couldn't miss the defeat in his voice. Once they were seated, Jennifer began, "What do you think about this weather?"

Troy turned to face her, and his lips curved into a slight smile. "Gee, Doc, don't you have something better in your bag of tricks?"

"Probably, but you've been in group long enough to know my best stuff."

"Doc, you're the coolest shrink I've ever met" Troy accented the comment with a wink.

Jennifer forced a smile for her client. "Thanks. I needed to hear that today."

"What's up? Your demons coming back to bite you in the ass, too?" Troy asked before sipping his coffee.

Jennifer responded without thinking. "Not really, just life. You think you've got it all mapped out, things appear good, then *boom* you're blindsided. Your whole world turns to shit."

The knots returned to her stomach. She stared at the floor and counted the spots in the square between her feet. It was hard to tell if the dots were original or had been created by years of built-up dirt, grime, and spilled coffee. Pondering their creation kept the growing defeat from swallowing her whole.

"So how does that make you feel?" Troy asked with a laugh.

"Still working that out." She let the silence hang but watched as her companion's body language tensed.

Gone was the brief smile. He crushed the empty Styrofoam cup in his palm, lowered his head, and the words came from a dark place. "The wife and I aren't doing good," Troy said, staring at the remains of the cup.

Knowing her client, Jennifer waited, didn't respond. She sipped the strong, over-brewed liquid.

"She can't look at what's left of my arm." He continued in a fragile and shaky tone. "The other night, she had too much to drink and called me Captain Hook. She has to be drunk on her ass before she'll let me touch her. The last time we made love, she was so wasted she called me the wrong name. I've known there's someone else, have for a while. This was verification."

Jennifer faced him and touched his shoulder. "You know I give it to you guys straight, right?" She heard the weariness that laced her tone.

"Yep, or I wouldn't be talking to you." His dark-eyed gaze met hers.

She leaned back in her chair and drew in a deep breath. "I understand. We hold up our end of the bargain, then those that say they love us toss us away like trash. Doesn't matter how it hurts; we're acceptable collateral damage." The dampness on her cheeks surprised her.

"Here," Troy said and handed her a napkin. "Take five, Doc. I'll gather the troops."

"Thanks." *Damn, what was wrong with her, sharing her feelings with a client and cursing? She'd embarrassed herself and Troy. Tears sent him running for cover. She had to shake this off. It was affecting her work.*

By the time everyone was seated, Jennifer had pulled herself together. She turned off the self-serving thoughts and focused on the group conversation. When the session ended, Troy remained to help straighten the room. "Doc, if you need anything, you can always count on the members of our group. You know we've got your back," he said, picking up a chair.

"Thanks, and Troy, make your own decisions. Decide what's best for you. Life's too short to allow people to treat you like crap. I apologize for earlier; I was out of line," Jennifer said, unplugging the coffee pot.

"Shows me you're human. It's all good." Troy shot her a smile.

She'd never be sure if it was his shadow, or she just knew he was there. She turned, and the sight of him took her breath away; his powerful well-muscled body moved with an easy grace as he closed the distance to her.

"Hello. Can I help you? Group's done for today. We meet again Thursday at two." Heat seemed to roll over her like dark clouds had parted above her on a rainy day.

"Hey, brother, I'll be done in a couple of minutes," Troy said, joining them.

A smile creased the stranger's face. "Need help?" he asked, still facing Jennifer.

"Nope. Jacks, this is Doc, officially, Colonel Ryan. I gotta take out the trash, be right back."

"Don't hurry on my account." Jacks shook Jennifer's hand. "Troy told me how helpful you've been, thanks."

Jennifer's mouth was dry, and she was struggling to catch her breath. Her face felt hot. "The sessions help me as much as the members. How long have you and Troy been friends?"

"Five years, give or take." The smile in his eyes held a sensuous flame.

She realized Jacks still held her hand, and pulled hers away. "It's good to have friends you can count on."

"Sure is. Maybe I'll join the group if you're in charge." He gave her a simple wink and slipped his hands into his jean pockets.

"Anyone is welcome," Jennifer said as she tucked a stray curl behind her ear.

He leaned in and whispered, "Never met an officer or shrink as beautiful as you."

Before Jennifer could respond, Troy returned. "Leave her alone, Casanova. Doc's way out of your league." He punched his friend on the shoulder.

"Nice meeting you," Jacks said as he flashed an irresistible grin.

She had her feet back under her and smiled. "Jacks, nice to meet you, too. Troy, I'll see you Thursday."

The pair walked a few steps toward the door. Troy stopped and returned, stepping so close Jennifer could smell the coffee on his breath. His hollow eyes locked with hers. "Doc, you need anything, and I mean *anything,* just ask. I owe you my life. There's nothing I wouldn't do if you asked. You understand, right?"

A shiver ran down Jennifer's spine like beads of sweat. Somehow, she found the voice to whisper, "Thanks, Troy."

****

Jennifer let out a long slow breath, "I hate this." Sweat coated her palms, and her heart was beating in time to a 1960s rock and roll tune. *A psychologist having a panic attack, Freud would have a field day with this.* The thought helped her relax, and she focused on the room, which didn't help. It was cold, painted in stark white, bleak, like her life. The room even smelled of cleaning materials.

Marion, her attorney, patted her client's hand. "It shouldn't take long. Unfortunately, it's part of the process." She motioned with her head toward the elevator, "That's Joseph Wilson, Phillip's attorney. I like this conference room; through the glass, I can check out the competition before they know I have them in my sights."

The stylishly dressed man was escorted to the conference room by the receptionist. His cold blue eyes focused directly on Jennifer from behind silver wire-rim glasses. His suit cost several thousand dollars if a dime. He wore a navy-blue bowtie with red polka dots; on anyone else, it would've looked comical, but he seemed to pull it off.

After introductions, Marion asked, "Your client isn't attending?"

"No," Joseph said in a sharp, curt tone.

Marion straightened her back. "Shall we get started?"

Mr. Wilson spoke as he removed a legal pad from his briefcase and a pen from his jacket pocket. He twisted the top of the gold fountain pen and said, "I requested this meeting to discuss the divorce settlement agreement between Mr. and Mrs. Ryan."

"I don't want a divorce," Jennifer quickly inserted.

Joseph continued as if she hadn't even spoken. "It's my hope we can come to an understanding. May I ask, Mrs. Ryan, why you insist on continuing a marriage when it's abundantly clear your husband does not?"

"I don't think he wants a divorce." Jennifer momentarily closed her eyes and fought to control her emotions; she wouldn't cry. "This affair will pass as did the last. Phillip and I made a commitment in front of God, our family, and friends. It shouldn't be thrown away, especially on a whim." She twisted her wedding band.

A calm settled over her as anger beat down the urge to cry. She leaned in and met Mr. Wilson's cold, hard stare. "There're the issues of time and money. Our daughters deserve a home with two parents who can provide the love and attention they need, as well as continue the same lifestyle. Not to mention I love my husband. Is that so difficult for you to comprehend, or are you only interested in legal facts?"

She watched the chill in Joseph's eyes, and the curve of his lips straightened. He placed his palms on the table. "You need to face reality, Mrs. Ryan. Your husband's moving forward. I suggest you consider your settlements options."

"Mr. Wilson, that's quite enough. We agreed to an

informal discussion, not provide you the opportunity to berate and harass my client," Marion said.

Jennifer touched Marion's arm. "Mr. Wilson, I'll discuss our meeting with my attorney and pastor."

He returned the legal pad to his briefcase and twisted the pen closed. "Can we set a meeting for Monday?"

After a long pause, Jennifer answered, "I suppose, but I'm not promising anything." Her stomach churned as she continued. "I'm not sure why Phillip's in such a hurry." Even though she knew, Jennifer wasn't ready to play that card.

"Speak with your pastor and consider the options. I apologize if I caused you any distress." He stood, and left the room.

His apology rang with insincerity and sarcasm. He was good at playing the attorney game, saying the right words with lackluster meaning. Were all men jerks?

With Joseph gone, Marion turned to her client. "Jennifer, we've been friends for years. You know I call things like I see them; I'm sorry, but it's my opinion. You need to accept the divorce is going to happen and decide on terms."

Jennifer stared at clenched hands in her lap. "What I want is my life the way it was before." She questioned the words before they were out of her mouth. Did she really, or was she grasping at memories that were marred with her interpretation and probably not accurate or even true?

Marion sipped her water before speaking. "Realistically, I don't think that's going to happen. Based on the investigator's report, we know two important facts. One, Lisa is pregnant, and two, her father, Adam Wallingford, has extremely deep pockets.

They're on the ropes; you can get what you want and then some."

"I know. I'll call you Thursday," Jennifer picked up her purse and left the office. She ducked into the ladies' room and leaned against the cold marble wall. Her world was slipping away, and there was nothing she could do, or was there?

****

Jennifer placed her empty cup on the parlor table. She and Pastor Bell had sipped tea and made small talk long enough. It was time for the serious conversation she'd come for.

In the past, the room helped her relax. The candles smelled of pumpkin, and a fire burned in the small fireplace. Today there was no comfort here; even her faith had been shaken by Phillip's actions. She was confused. She steeled her roller coaster of emotions. "What do you think I should do, give up and let Phillip go?"

Pastor Bell leaned back in his chair, his fingers arched together, and spoke with quiet emphasis. "I think you've done everything you can. This is the third time Phillip has committed adultery, that you know about, anyway. His actions free you from all commitments you made to him in the eyes of God. I never encourage divorce, but think about this; don't you deserve a husband who loves and respects you, a man who'll put you first?"

Jennifer took a deep breath, leaned forward, and placed her folded hands on the desk. "Phillip's attorney asked for my list of settlement demands. Marion thinks I should accept the divorce is going to happen."

"I think you should consider her suggestion.

However, if you aren't ready to end your marriage, perhaps if you make your demands difficult enough, Phillip might take time to think the divorce through. It's a decision only you can make."

"Thank you," Jennifer said and stood.

As the pastor helped Jennifer with her coat, he continued, "Either way, you and the girls will get through this. Remember, I'm always here for you, no matter what your decision."

"Thank you. The girls and I'll see you Sunday." Jennifer left the church, removed her cell phone from her purse, and dialed Marion's number. Her assistant put her through.

"Hello, Jennifer," Marion said.

"I'm going to put together my list of conditions. If Phillip will agree, I'll sign the final papers. You'll have my email tonight."

"Okay, if I have questions, I'll call. If not, we can meet prior to the settlement conference Monday," her attorney said.

"Do I have to attend?" Jennifer fought the growing panic.

"Not unless you want to."

"Good," Jennifer said, climbing into her car. "I don't think I can sit quietly as the end of my marriage is negotiated like a business deal. There'll be no changes to my demands. It's all or nothing." Jennifer ended the call, dropped the phone in her purse, turned up the country station, and let her head rest on the seat back. It was time to consider Plan B and what that would mean for her daughters.

Chapter Two

Jennifer was lost in thought as she drove toward the hospital. Three clients were scheduled for the afternoon. She was contemplating materials for a new dachshund quilt when she felt the bump, then another. *Damn. A flat tire.*

She pulled to the shoulder, pounded the steering wheel, and let her head fall forward. "What else could possibly go wrong today? Why did I wear a skirt?" she shouted to the universe.

She was opening the hatch when a motorcycle pulled in behind her car. She turned and watched the man climb from the bike, which he carried out with one swift move of his long leg.

He removed his helmet and placed it on the bike handle. It was Jacks. He reached inside his jacket, retrieved a pair of sunglasses, and slipped them on. Pulled a baseball cap from his back pocket, snapped it open, and slipped it on in a well-practiced motion.

As he covered the space between them, she couldn't miss the broad shoulders and the confident swagger. She let out a sigh. He was a very fine specimen of a hot, sexy man.

"Afternoon, Doc," he said with a nod of his head. "What a pleasant surprise. Good to see you again." His smile was broad, playful, and a bit mischievous.

"Good to see you as well. How you are?"

"Better now." His smile sent her sexual desire off the charts. "May I change your tire?" He held up both hands and quickly added, "I'm sure you can do it, but I'd consider it my good deed for the day." His voice was deep and smoky.

"That would be very nice. I'm not exactly dressed for changing it." Jennifer bit her lip to stop a goofy smile. She didn't miss his obvious examination and approval.

He held out his hand, "Troy didn't officially introduce me. I'm Jackson Williams, but my friends call me Jacks." He slipped off the jacket and placed it on the hatch.

"Jennifer." She shook his hand before she continued, "Thanks for stopping. A flat tire is icing on the cake of a not-so-wonderful day."

"When we're done here, I'll buy you a beer. You can tell me all about it," he suggested and gave her a smile that sent her pulse racing.

"Sorry. I have clients at the clinic this afternoon." She rubbed the back of her neck. Why was she so nervous? Suddenly she didn't know what to do with her hands.

"I'll take a rain check," he said, adding a sexy grin.

She rolled her eyes, smiled, and felt her face blush as she took in the full picture. He had a day's growth of beard, sandy-colored hair, cut in the military high and tight, and a devilishly handsome face.

As he loosened the lug nuts, his muscles rippled under his white T-shirt. She leaned back a bit and let her eyes wander downward until she had a clear view of his denim-covered butt, and a fine one it was. There was a tingling in the pit of her stomach.

Stop it. You're checking him out like you're in heat.

17

She hid her smile. *What was wrong with her letting the handsome sailor melt her with his eyes? Sending her into sexual overdrive, what the hell?*

****

Jacks drank in his second look at the attractive Air Force officer. Her lips were full and round, the kind a man could enjoy for a very long time. The visual tour from the high heels to the hem of her skirt and back again was exceptional. The tailored blouse encased round, full breasts.

Concentrate on changing the tire, he scolded himself after his hand slipped and he scraped his knuckles for the third time. But that was quickly forgotten as his thoughts drifted to taking down her hair one pin at a time, and all the things he'd like to do with her had his imagination and libido raging.

It had been way too long since he'd been alone with a woman. Thanks to his ex-wife, he hadn't been in the mood to open up and trust, but he was past the one-night stand. Perhaps it was time to start looking for someone.

The two engaged in small talk until he stood and brushed his hands together. "There you go, all done."

"Thanks. What do I owe you?" Jennifer asked as she handed him his jacket and closed the hatch.

Jacks leaned against the jeep, crossed his ankles, and slipped his hands into his pockets. "It was my pleasure. If I can't buy you a beer, how about giving me your phone number? I'm here on temporary duty, again. Troy's fishing with friends. I'm free all weekend."

Jennifer grinned, and her dimples sent a bolt of lust through his body. "I think you'll have lots of friends in very short order, good-looking sailor like yourself."

"How can you be so sure I'm a sailor?"

18

She grinned and looked over the top of her sunglasses. "I have several friends who are squids. They have the same cocky attitude."

"Good cocky?"

"Most of the time, good seeing you again," she said in a controlled tone.

He picked up on the joking sound in her words. Placed his hand over his heart and teased, "My ego will be forever bruised."

Jennifer shook her head and chuckled. "Go to the club on base. I'm sure you'll be in love in five minutes."

"Afternoon, Colonel, it was indeed a pleasure." *A pleasure indeed.* Another chance encounter certainly stirred his emotions and sexual desire. A man could make a hobby out of working his way up and down Jennifer Ryan's tight shapely legs. He'd have to keep an eye out for this sexy creature. She'd stirred his interest and flamed his sexual desire again.

****

Jennifer logged onto her email account and opened the inbox. The first message was from Marion. She steeled her nerves, hovered the cursor over the message, and clicked open. The words jumped from the page.

I met with Mr. Wilson. Phillip will meet your conditions. I know this is what we expected, but as we discussed, Phillip's financial backer has deep pockets and a great deal of political clout. Judge Marcus has tentatively approved the child support amount. I also expect a quick court date. But for that to happen, the affair will become public record, given adultery is the only condition under which Virginia divorce laws allow the one-year waiting period to be waived. Attached is a rough draft of the settlement documents. Review the documents and get back with me.

She opened the document and began to read... *in the matter of the marriage of Phillip M. Ryan, Plaintiff and Jennifer L. Ryan, Defendant, blah, blah, blah.* She scrolled to the second page and skimmed the neatly typed words; she rested her chin in her palm as she read.

Her eyes darted from line to line. Jennifer forced herself to slow down, carefully taking in the meaning of each numbered item. *Plaintiff will, prior to signing of the final decree of divorce: (1) Pay in full all marital debt including the mortgage for the current family residence and sign a Quit Claim Deed to Plaintiff; (2) Deposit three hundred twenty-five thousand dollars into Defendant's trust account; (3) Set up direct deposit payments of Child Support in the amount of four thousand dollars per month. Child Support payments will continue, with an annual two point five percent increase, until the children have completed their college degrees to include all graduate studies. At which time the monthly payments will be deposited into Defendant's retirement account; (4) Plaintiff will maintain a five-million-dollar life insurance policy with Defendant as sole beneficiary.*

The rest of the document addressed Phillip's financial responsibilities with regard to the children's medical and dental insurance, tuition for private school and college, and extra-curricular activities.

Jennifer will retain sole custody of their daughters. Plaintiff will deposit into the trust in the amount equal to two years of payments prior to the execution of the final dissolution of marriage. The account will be funded monthly through direct deposit. The visitation schedule is attached.

She lowered her head and let the tears come. After twenty years, it would come down to dollars and cents.

****

Jennifer was selecting moon drop grapes when she saw Jacks. His steps seem to quicken when he noticed her. There wasn't a place to retreat. A flush of adrenaline sent tingles through her body. The man made her breathless and her heart race.

"Afternoon, Colonel, we meet again. It must be fate." His words were soft as a caress. Jacks extended his hand, and when she took it, he closed both of his hands around hers. His half nod and grin sent a warm rush through her body.

"How are you this afternoon?" she somehow managed to mumble. He looked sexier in the flight suit than in jeans. Without his sunglasses, she could see his eyes were warm golden brown with flecks of green. His smile made her feel uncomfortable yet excited at the same time.

"Better now that I've run into you." Without skipping a beat, he continued, "What brings Air Force into Navy territory?"

She reluctantly slid her hand from his and pulled a plastic bag from the roll. "I covered for a colleague at the base hospital intake clinic today."

"Perhaps fate is on my side after all," Jacks said and picked up grapes before he leaned in and said, "Seriously, thanks for your work with Troy."

She fumbled trying to put the grapes in a bag. "He's doing all the work. It was nice seeing you, I need to finish shopping, and pick up my daughters. She felt jumpy and flushed. *What's wrong with me I can't even carry on a conversation?*

21

"I'll shop with you," Jacks said.

Jennifer saw no way out; he didn't appear to be in a hurry to leave her alone.

"Tell me about your daughters?" Jacks asked, grabbing a small watermelon as they paused at the display.

She smiled. *Telling him about my girls will send him running.* "They're fourteen-year-old twins." She pushed her cart to the first aisle.

He picked up a cantaloupe, examined it and set it in his basket. "Must keep you busy."

"It does, between school, sports, and church, sometimes I feel like a taxi driver." She looked at her grocery list and tried to focus, do anything to stop thinking how amazing his hands would feel on her body.

Jacks moved in tandem up and down the aisles. Twice he reached across her arm to grab an item. His scent was all male, soap, sunshine, and a hint of leather.

At the checkout, Jennifer announced, a bit too loudly, "I'm done. It was nice seeing you again." For some reason, she couldn't stand still. She straightened her uniform jacket for something to do with her hands.

"It was nice shopping with you." He touched her arm. "By the way, I went to the O-Club, didn't fall in love," she caught a gleam of mischievousness in his sexy wink.

Her pulse raced, and her stomach fluttered. "Sorry. I hear that's quite the place to go." Now she was playing with her hair. Could she be any lamer?

"Give me your phone number?" His killer smile and bright, sparkling eyes caused her heart to beat faster.

Her response spilled out too fast. For some reason, she couldn't remove her eyes from his gaze. "Jacks, you seem to be a nice guy, but I'm married. That's until the judge signs the final divorce papers next week. I really don't have time for a man in my life, especially a young pilot."

Jacks stepped in closer. "I'm not that young," he whispered and allowed the sexy grin to fill his face.

His warm breath crept over her cheek; she felt the heat rise from her toes to the top of her head. "I really have to go." Panic laced her voice. What was wrong with her?

He placed his hand beside hers on the cart; the touch was electric. He continued in the hushed tone. "Before you go, can I ask you something?"

"Okay," she replied, trying to break the spell he'd woven her in.

"What color are your eyes?" He stroked her knuckle with his thumb.

"Lavender." She was sweating, her heart was pounding in her throat, and she wanted to kiss him.

"I've never met anyone with lavender eyes." He stepped even closer and slid a loose curl behind her ear.

She licked her lips. "I get that all the time. Have a nice afternoon," she said and made her way to the register as quickly as possible. She felt like a fickle teenager fleeing the scene of a crime.

****

Jennifer flipped the switch on the robotic sweeper and set it loose to attack the living room floor. At least she'd begin her new life as a single mom with a house cleaned from top to bottom. Tomorrow her marriage would be over. All that remained was a short appearance in the judge's chambers and signatures on the final decree. Just like that, it would be over, twenty years thrown away, like a pair of old, comfortable shoes.

She sipped the glass of cranberry juice with a large amount of vodka. Alcohol never solved problems, but one drink was all she needed to help her fall asleep. The second seemed to be doing the trick quicker. A soft knock at the front door stopped her from sitting at the kitchen island.

She placed her drink on the counter and headed to the door. Through the peep hole, she saw Phillip. She placed her forehead on the door, counted to ten, took a deep breath, and opened the door. "What are you doing here?" she asked, letting all the hostility of the day pour out.

"I wanted to make sure you're okay."

She laughed and replied in cold sarcasm. "Oh, I'm just fucking peachy! How about you?" Tension attacked what had been relaxed shoulders.

He stepped closer. "Have you been drinking?"

She backed from his reach, and threw her hands in the air. "I have, but what business is it of yours?"

"You never drink." He smiled and reached for her again.

"Thank you very much for your concern. We'll be divorced tomorrow. No need to worry; I'll show up for the hearing." She stepped back to close the door but for some reason, stopped when he spoke. His voice was gentle and kind, like in the first years of their marriage—before she discovered he was a lying, cheating bastard.

"You'll always be my concern. Just because we're divorcing won't change that. Sweetheart, you were my first true love," Phillip said, brushing his fingertips across her cheek, down her neck, coming to rest at the base of her skull.

As he leaned in to kiss her, Jennifer's mind was screaming *Stop!* but she couldn't. Her body ached to be touched. She wanted to feel desired again, not the wife tossed over for a younger woman. Tomorrow she'd blame it on the booze or, better yet, justify it as a Freudian defense mechanism.

He gently nudged her to him. "Kiss me," he whispered.

She stepped into his arms and forgot everything. It felt good to be wanted even if it was only an illusion. It was just sex, after all.

Phillip shut the door and led her down the hall to what had been their bedroom. They kissed and touched like they had as teenagers all those years ago in the back seat of his car. Except this time, they knew exactly how to please each other.

He'd taught, and she'd learned. Phillip lay back, and Jennifer used those talents. She gave a sexual performance he'd never forget, one to which there'd never be an encore. She left him struggling to catch his breath and composure.

They slept curled together. She wasn't sure what time it was but felt the light brush of his lips on her cheek and heard the whisper, "I'll always love you."

She pretended to sleep as he dressed and listened as his footsteps echoed down the hall. For the first time since he'd moved out, she allowed herself to cry. She wasn't really sure why. Her inner therapist whispered, "It's natural to grieve the death of your marriage, no matter what your true feelings."

****

At three o'clock sharp, the judge signed the divorce decree; Jennifer was officially a single mother of two.

Fall leaves crunched under her feet as she crossed the parking lot and climbed into her car. There were no tears. As over the last several months, her emotions were still a whirl as she pulled into what was now her garage.

She changed into dachshund pajamas, poured a glass of wine, and removed the divorce paperwork from her purse. She sat in the overstuffed chair, propped her feet on the ottoman, opened the paperwork, sipped her wine, and smiled just a bit.

Phillip Ryan had tossed her aside; she had and would continue to deal with the pain associated with it, but it was getting easier every day. He was no longer her concern, and she was a very wealthy woman. All in all, she'd come out the other side okay, maybe even able to see a positive light at the end of the tunnel. She was equally sure the light was not the proverbial train.

Chapter Three

The large heron high-stepped along the riverbank. The graceful bird was in search of breakfast. Jennifer sipped her coffee and scanned the yard for other morning visitors. It had been an emotional year. The renovation of the turn of the century river house had taken longer than expected, but their new home had finally come together.

The warm breeze caused the moss to dance in the oak trees. Birds darted from tree to bush; she'd have to fill the bird feeders again. A lone whitetail deer stood silently at the water's edge.

She moved across the balcony and surveyed the yard; the vegetable and herb gardens were in full bloom. The last rounds of vegetables for the season were about ready to harvest. She smiled, recalling the canning she and the twins had done.

Purple geranium and hibiscus blooms greeted visitors along the walk. Squirrels played tag around the pinecone lilies, peeking from the mulched bed announcing fall was on the way.

More importantly, the twins were adjusting to seeing their father on weekends and building a relationship with Lisa. Like the house, Jennifer's emotions had settled into a sense of normal. She still had her moments, but the girls seemed happy, and that's what really mattered.

She headed to the kitchen, refilled her cup with the dark roast New Orleans chicory coffee, and saw Phillip's car pull into the driveway. "Girls, your father and Lisa are here."

Jennifer met Phillip halfway between the car and the house, smiled, and asked, "Would you and Lisa like to come in?"

He slipped his hands into his front pockets. "I don't think she's ready for that yet."

She chuckled and said, "Seriously. I'm the one who should be pissed. She seduced my husband and ruined my marriage. Help the girls with their things." She walked past Phillip and headed toward the car.

Jennifer smiled as she peered in the car window. Lisa looked scared to death. *What does she think—I'm planning to kill her? If she only knew how happy I am she has the jerk.*

She folded her arms on the open car window and leaned in. "Hey, Lisa, how are you feeling? How's Phillip Junior?" Lisa looked so young, dainty, and small. Her blonde hair was cut in a shag. Phillip's favorite style. He loved being in control. Jennifer hadn't known how much until they weren't living together. The signs of manipulation were there, but she'd missed them, too.

"We're both fine, and you?" Lisa's voice seemed to waiver.

"I'm doing well. I think it's time we worked on being friends. It would make things easier for the girls. I presume you'll come to games, recitals, and the like. They'd appreciate it if you would. It'll be good if we let the past go; I can."

This time Lisa's voice was stronger but guarded. "That would be nice."

28

"Wonderful, I hope you and Phillip will come to their birthday party. Let your father know he's invited, too. I think the girls have adopted him as an unofficial grandfather.

Jennifer watched the scared facial expression fade. "I'll check with Phillip. I could help. Dad really enjoys when the girls visit."

"Good. I know the girls would love it if everyone attended. We'll have lunch and plan, make a day of it. It might be a bit awkward at first, but we'll work through the weirdness."

"Here we are," Phillip said opening the car door and the girls climbed in.

Jennifer flashed her best guess-what-I-did smile. It would give Phillip something to wonder about, which gave her a great sense of satisfaction.

"Girls, enjoy your visit and help Miss Lisa; I'll see you Tuesday at school."

"Okay, Mom. Love you," both girls chimed from the back seat.

"Lisa, talk to Phillip about the girl's birthday party, and get back to me."

Jennifer waved as the car pulled from the driveway. It would be nice to be a fly on the wall for the discussion between them about the upcoming birthday.

Before Jennifer reached the porch, her cell phone rang. She sat on the porch step and answered.

"Hey, girlfriend, what's up?" Kimberly asked.

Her best friend's voice made Jennifer smile. "The girls just left for a long weekend with their dad."

"Good, you can join us."

"What do you have going on now?" *It would be a party; she'd use any excuse to throw one.*

29

"Three of Brandon's friends transferred into Norfolk Naval. Two are staying at the house. We're having an impromptu cookout; would you like to join the fun?"

"Why not? What can I bring?" Jennifer drew lines in the dirt of the potted fern beside her.

"I was hoping you'd keep me company while I shop."

"I can do that. You going to the commissary?" Jennifer asked as she turned the potted fern to face the sun.

"Yep, how about in an hour?"

"See you there," Jennifer said. She remained on the porch enjoying the cool breeze and watching the fat blue jays attack the feeder and suet. It was time for her to step into life and see what the future held; she'd been living life through her children long enough. Plus, there was always an excess of unattached men at Kimberly's parties.

She could drink, laugh, flirt, and maybe find a date for the next night the girls were visiting their dad. Dread hit her squarely between the eyes. She hadn't been on a date in over twenty years. She momentarily considered hiding out a little longer.

"All right, scaredy cat, get your butt moving," she said to the universe and headed inside.

****

Jennifer followed Kimberly through the neighborhood and parked behind her SUV. They'd tried to buy out the commissary, her car was loaded with the overflow that wouldn't fit in her friend's car. Brandon and several men were sitting on the porch sipping drinks and smoking cigars.

"There're tons of bags in the cars. We have enough food to feed a small army," Kimberly said to the group as she and Jennifer reached the porch.

"That's good. Our guests are growing in number," Brandon said, heading down the steps, kissing his wife, and hugging Jennifer. "Hey, good looking. Thanks for helping with the shopping. I wasn't looking forward to going there."

"No problem, visiting you two is always fun, and we both know Kimberly can throw a party."

"What do we have to cook?" Brandon asked, holding Jennifer at arms' length.

"Chicken, ribs, and steaks, plus anything else we saw that looked good."

"Jennifer's going to bake your favorite Irish Car Bomb cupcakes," Kimberly whispered to her husband.

"I might be in love," he chuckled and hugged Jennifer again. "How are you really?" he asked in a hushed tone before he stepped back.

She shrugged before answering, "I'm hanging in."

"Well, you look good." He took her hand and led her to the porch. "Gentlemen, it's my pleasure to introduce psychologist extraordinaire, Dr. Jennifer Ryan. She introduced me to my lovely wife. Jennifer, I think you know most everyone except Mike and Jacks."

Jennifer flashed Jacks a knowing smile.

"For the record, Jacks, she's single, available, and is the only woman I know who doesn't complain about cigar smoke. Occasionally, she'll even smoke one. Oh, and she loves scotch on the rocks."

"Nice to meet you both," Jennifer said. "Brandon, why don't you put a singles advertisement online?"

"Give me the word, and it will be done, my lady,"

Brandon said and let out a booming laugh.

She grinned at Jacks' smile. "So, we meet again," he said, descending the stairs.

"Yes, it appears we do." Her breath quickened as he approached.

"You two know each other?" Brandon asked.

"He changed my tire sometime last year," Jennifer fought to calm her voice.

He took her hand in his. "That was our first date. The second, if I recall correctly, was the commissary. She left me standing at the checkout, no phone number, nothing." His gaze was soft as a caress.

Jennifer rolled her eyes. "Please, I'm sure you were heartbroken."

"My dear, you have no idea, but we can discuss it over a drink."

****

Jennifer wiggled her toes in the pool. She and Kimberly sat side by side in chair floats.

"So, what do you think of Jacks?" Kimberly asked, swirling her wine before taking a sip.

"I just met him. What opinion can I have? What do you think of this weather?" She responded quickly, trying to derail the conversation. "You have to love Hampton Roads, seventy-eight degrees today, and by Monday, it'll be snowing." Jennifer closed her eyes and pictured Jacks' hands stroking her face.

"Stop trying to change the subject. What I was asking about is the view," Kimberly smiled and motioned with her glass toward Jacks.

Jennifer looked at the group playing volleyball and took a second before she answered, "He's certainly easy to look at with those green eyes and sandy blond hair, I'll give you that."

"Like you didn't notice those six-pack abs and tight ass?" Kimberly whispered and laughed.

"No. I didn't miss those at all or his tanned, toned biceps. I'm divorced, not dead. I'm sure being tangled up with a divorced mother of teenage girls is what he's looking for. He's a pilot. No doubt there's a long line of single ladies waiting in the wings."

"Actually, his marriage to a blonde bimbo broke up about a year ago. He's recovering and moving slowly. Wait, does that sound like someone else I know?" Kimberly turned to face her friend.

Jennifer sipped her wine. "I'm not ready to become someone's lover. The only man I've had sex with was Phillip. On a psychological level, I understand the reason he cheated had nothing to do with me, but as a woman, it hurts like hell."

"What was it he told you? Wait, I know," Kimberly said, using her left hand to paddle closer to Jennifer. "Sweetheart, it's not you. I need variety," Kimberly added with a chuckle.

Jennifer touched her glass to Kimberly's. "Yes. I guess he was trying to make me feel better."

"We both know he wants back in your bed; all you have to do is whistle."

"I won't do that to Lisa, even though it would give me great satisfaction. She'll figure things out on her own. Phillip came by the night before we went to court. We had some fun."

"What?" Kimberly said, almost choking on her wine.

Jennifer laughed out loud at the way Kimberly's head snapped toward her. She sipped her wine before continuing. "Technically, he was still my husband, and I was in the mood. I wanted him to remember what he'd never have again. I must say I put on quite the performance. Perhaps he thought taking me to bed would soften the blow, but as we know, I got the last laugh."

"That you certainly did," Kimberly said and held her glass up in a toast.

And you only know the half of it, my friend. Jennifer's thoughts were interrupted.

"Look out in the pool," someone yelled as several players from the volleyball game cannon balled into the water.

The splash flipped Kimberly's float. Jennifer was shoved toward the other end of the pool before hers overturned. As she surfaced, warm liquid ran down her face. She wiped it away; her hand was covered in blood. She swam toward the ladder and climbed out.

No one seemed to notice her injury but Jacks. As she climbed from the pool, she saw him running in her direction. He picked up a towel, was by her side in seconds, and led her to a chair.

"Sit down and put your head back." He pressed the towel tight against the wound.

"Brandon, Jennifer's hurt," Jacks yelled. The tone in his voice caught everyone's attention.

"What happened?" Brandon asked when he reached them.

"The chair flipped. I cut my head on the metal arm. Maybe I hit the side of the pool. Or broke my wine glass, I'm not sure."

"Let me look at your head. Brandon, I told you those old floats needed to go," Kimberly said. Her aggravation coated her tone.

Jacks removed the towel; Kimberly checked the wound. As soon as the compress was removed, blood streamed down Jennifer's face. "That's going to need stitches. Come on, I'll drive you to the hospital."

"I need to get dressed. I can't go to the hospital in a swimsuit," Jennifer said, standing.

"Put this on," Jacks said, handing her a T-shirt. He shifted the towel as she did. The jersey dwarfed her; it fell below her knees.

"Thanks."

"Can you hold the towel?" Jacks asked.

"Sure."

"Good, keep as much pressure on it as you can," he said and scooped her into his arms.

"I'm fine. You don't need to carry me." She could feel the primal heat surging through her body. Automatically, she ran her arm around his neck.

"Hush and let me be the hero, will you?" he said with a wink.

"Kimberly, I need my purse," Jennifer said over Jacks' shoulder.

"Bring a few more towels too," Jacks added, turning slightly.

He placed Jennifer in the back seat and climbed in beside her. Kimberly got in a moment later, started the car, and headed to Langley Medical Center.

"How are you feeling?" Jacks asked as he slid his left arm around the back of Jennifer's seat.

"My head's beginning to hurt, and my vision is a bit blurry. Must be a pretty good-sized cut," Jennifer added, rubbing her index finger up her nose and between her eyes.

"More like a gash," Kimberly said, making eye

contact in the rearview mirror. She stopped in front of the emergency room door. "Go on in. I'll park and find you."

"Okay." Jacks helped Jennifer from the car and scooped her up again.

"I can walk." She could, but it felt warm in his arms, maybe too warm.

"Sure, you can. But it'll be more romantic to tell our kids I carried you into the emergency room, especially after you got hurt trying to get my attention." He laughed.

"I must really be hurt. What did you say?" Jennifer asked as she ringed her arms around his neck.

"You heard me, beautiful. Okay, here's the plan: act like you're really hurt, and we can get you patched up and back to the party. I want to spend time getting to know you. This isn't quite what I had in mind for our next date."

"Okay, that works," Jennifer said as warning signals were clanging in her ears. Jacks was not for her. He was way too young and only looking for a fling. She could enjoy the distraction, take him to bed, and enjoy. Jennifer mentally shook her head. What the hell was she thinking? The injury was affecting her normal, practical thought process. She smiled just a bit, well maybe —her thought was cut short by another voice.

Chapter Four

"Can I help you?" the airman asked at the reception desk.

"The colonel hit her head in the pool. She's bleeding, is in pain, light-headed, and her vision is blurred."

"You can put me down anytime," Jennifer said. But it was a halfhearted request. She felt pleasure having someone fuss over her for a change.

Before he could respond, the airman said, "Sir, carry your wife into exam room three. It's down the hall on the left. Someone will be right in. Do you have her military identification?"

"No, but I do," Kimberly said, approaching the desk.

"I'll take it. We'll get the paperwork started," the airman responded.

Jennifer looked up at Jacks, grinned, and said, "All right, dear, you heard the airman."

"Right away, darling." He carried her into the examination room and sat her on the table.

A nurse entered behind them. "Hello, ma'am, I'm Captain Bishop. I'll be handling your preliminary exam. Please lie back." She removed the towel, opened a sterile compress, and applied it to the gash.

"What happened?"

"I was sitting on a float in the pool, and it overturned. I'm not sure exactly how I cut my head,"

Jennifer said.

"Keep the bandage pressed firmly against the wound. Did you lose consciousness?"

"No."

The efficient but not too friendly nurse checked Jennifer's vitals and completed the necessary forms with few words. "The doctor will be right in."

Jacks tucked a stray curl behind Jennifer's ear. "She certainly was a ray of sunshine. I wouldn't want her to give me a sponge bath," he said with a snicker.

Before she could reply, Captain Larsen rushed into the room, "Jennifer, Colonel, what happened? I hoped it was a mistake when the nurse handed me your chart."

"I'm fine, probably need stitches."

"Kimberly, Jacks, this is Captain Toby Larsen. He is the best emergency room doctor I know," she paused briefly, "but I don't know that many." She laughed and winked at Toby.

"Thank you so much for the wonderful introduction and vote of confidence."

"Toby, these are my friends Kimberly and Jacks."

"Hello. Jennifer, if you're done with the comedy routine, I'll take a look," he said as they shook hands. "Would you wait outside while I examine the colonel?" Toby asked.

"Kimberly and I will be in the hall if you need anything," Jacks said, exiting the room.

"What happened?" The captain asked.

Jennifer explained the events as he took her pulse. "I'm sure it's nothing a few stitches won't fix," she said.

He listened to her heart and lungs. "Did you lose consciousness?"

"No, I have a slight headache," she said, rubbing the

top of her head.

Toby checked her pupils with a pen light. "Everything seems okay so far. Let me take a look at the injury." He lifted the bandage and replaced it with a new one.

"Stitches for sure. What's today's date?"

"Seriously?" Jennifer asked, shaking her head.

"You know the protocol."

"Okay, it's Saturday, the fifteenth."

"Any memory loss?"

"What's your name again?"

Toby ignored her comment and held out his hands, palm side down. Three fingers on each hand extended. "Squeeze my fingers."

Jennifer clamped down on Toby's fingers like vises. "You okay," she asked when he winced.

"Great." He took her hand and helped her from the table.

"Put me through the paces, Romberg test, right? Jennifer asked.

"Yes, Colonel Smarty Pants," the captain said and slipped his hands into his coat pockets.

Jennifer went through the balance exercises, answered his questions, and took a bow.

Toby waved with his left hand. "Come sit down. You might want to be nice to me. I'm going to stitch you up and order an MRI." He held up his index finger when Jennifer began to speak. "Just to be safe." Toby sat on the small rolling stool and steepled his fingers. "Or if you would rather spend the night in the hospital, I can arrange it."

"MRI it is," Jennifer said, rubbing her hands together.

"I'll get your friends," Captain Larsen said and stepped into the hall. "She's going to be fine. You can go back in."

"Hello, again," Jacks said and placed his hand over hers.

"Hello, sweetheart. What, no roses?" Jennifer winked and smiled.

"I'll save that for our fourth date." His smile and caress made her feel safe and protected.

"What's going on with you two?" Kimberly asked

"Sorry, it's an inside joke that got started when the nurse told Jacks to carry his wife into the exam room."

Kimberly sat in a corner chair. "I guess if I leave you two alone for five minutes, I'll be a godmother again." She laughed and continued. "What's the plan?"

"Stitches and an MRI," Jennifer said and pulled a blanket over her legs.

Jacks placed his left hand on the table and leaned in. "You, okay? Anything I can do to help?" His eyes were compelling, magnetic.

Kiss me, popped into Jennifer's head. Instead, she mumbled, "No. I'm good." She wanted to crawl into his arms and never let go. Sexual tension pulsed through Jennifer; her breath quickened.

A devilish grin slowly grew on his lips. The shadow of his slight beard only contributed to his manly aura.

Kimberly broke the spell, "Come on, Jacks, I need coffee. Let the doctor get things rolling."

"It won't be long. Rank has its privileges," Toby said, patting Jennifer on the hand.

"We'll check back. Jennifer, you want a sandwich or anything?" Jacks asked as he brushed loose curls from the bandage.

"I'm good, but thanks." Jennifer relaxed on the table and closed her eyes. When Jacks was nearby, the air around her seemed electrified, and along with it came an unwelcomed surge of sexual excitement. What was it about him? It had to be because it had been a long time since a man paid attention to her. Sexual deprivation, that's all it was. Wasn't it?

****

Jacks and Kimberly strolled to the cafeteria. His stomach was turning somersaults. He had trouble sitting still and played with his coffee cup more than drank from it.

"What's up?" Kimberly asked before nibbling on the cookie Jacks had bought.

"I guess. No. Hell, I don't know." *What the hell's wrong with me? I don't even know this woman; she has my stomach in knots. Where had this overprotective streak come from?*

Kimberly reached across the table and touched her fingers to his. "She'll be okay."

"I know, it's just, damn, Jennifer's—oh, never mind." He breathed a sigh of relief when Kimberly changed the subject.

"You've known Brandon for a long time?" Kimberly asked.

Jacks smiled, his internal control returning. "All my life—back in the day, he and Dad were helicopter pilot and co-pilot. I think Brandon joined the service about six years after my dad. Our families were stationed in many of the same places. I grew up hanging out at their house and his kids at ours. Dorothy was like a second mother." Jacks sipped the coffee. "Sorry, does talking about her make you uncomfortable?"

41

"Only because I understand she was a wonderful person and wife. It's hard to fill her shoes. Don't get me wrong, I'm not jealous. I hope I'll always make Brandon happy. Sometimes I worry about his kids and how to build a strong relationship with them."

He smiled, leaned in, and whispered, "I'll let you in on a little secret—Brandon's kids love you."

Kimberly smiled before responding. "Thanks for telling me. I worry sometimes they don't since Brandon and I got together less than a year after their mom died."

"You don't have to worry. All four have told me they're glad you two are together."

"Good, thanks for sharing that." She continued after a short pause, "Are you ready for the deployment?"

"Getting there, we'll be doing nighttime touch and go's next week."

"What was it Brandon says about landing on an aircraft carrier at night?"

Jacks looked left, then right, leaned closer, and whispered. "I bet I know. The three best things in life are a good landing, a good orgasm, and a good shit. A night carrier landing is one of the few opportunities to experience all three at one time. Excuse the language."

Kimberly's laugh made him smile. "That would be it."

Jacks looked at his watch.

"You ready to head back?" Kimberly asked and smiled.

"Sure." Jacks stopped outside the gift shop. "Hang on." He selected a single yellow rose from the cooler and paid for it.

"What's up?" Kimberly asked when he returned.

"Not sure. Jennifer gets my strange sense of humor.

I want to get to know her." At the same time, it scared the shit out of him. This woman had haunted his mind and dreams since the day he'd met her. It was her face he saw when he pleasured himself. He wanted to get as far away from her as he could but knew it wouldn't do any good. He had to see where this was going; panic hit. He was glad they'd reached the waiting room. He needed to sit down. *People don't fall in love like this. Do they?*

Kimberly's voice pulled him back. "Did you know yellow roses are her favorite?"

Before he could respond, Toby wheeled Jennifer into the waiting room. "Our patient's ready to go."

Jacks pushed the thoughts away, handed her the rose, and smiled. When their eyes met, he wanted to pull her into his arms, hold her close, protect her. Damn, he wanted, hell, needed, to kiss her, taste her.

"Thanks, dear," Jennifer responded before she smelled the rose.

"She needs to take it easy for a few days, no driving for twenty-four hours. She has her prescriptions and items for wound care," Toby said.

Jennifer shook the paper bag in her lap. "Thanks, Toby. I'll see you Wednesday for the follow-up."

"Take it easy," he responded.

"Will do."

"You're going to spend the next couple of days at my house. I need to keep an eye on you and don't even try to argue," Kimberly said and held up her index finger.

"I wouldn't even think about it, but I need a few things from my house."

"No problem. Jacks, you don't mind a short side trip, do you?" Kimberly asked.

"Not at all. I'm along for the company." Yep, it was

good he was deploying soon. He'd be forced to put some distance between him and this woman who appeared to have captured his heart.

****

As they turned onto the drive, Jennifer said, "Welcome to my hideaway."

"This is wonderful. Are you on the water?" Jacks asked.

"Yes, the Chesapeake Bay. There's always a remarkable sunset."

"How long have you lived here?" Jacks asked as he took Jennifer's hand and helped her from the jeep.

"A little over a year."

Once inside, Jennifer said, "There're all sorts of things in the refrigerator to drink. Glasses are in the cabinet beside the wine refrigerator. Help yourself."

"Thanks."

"Sweetie, would you like some help?" Kimberly asked.

"Yes, please," she answered, heading upstairs.

Jennifer removed and handed the T-shirt to her friend. "This needs to be laundered, and soon, there's quite a bit of blood on it."

"We'll take it with us; I'll spray it and put it in the wash. What does this say? *Newton's Law states that what goes up must come down. Our Company Commander's Law states that what goes up and comes down had damn well better be able to go back up again.*" Kimberly snickered.

"I'm not sure who the shirt belongs to," Jennifer said, removing her swimsuit and hanging it in the shower.

"I'm pretty sure it belongs to Jacks; it appears he's

interested in you."

Jennifer caught the way Kimberly raised her eyebrows. "Please. As we discussed, I'm not his type."

"Will you at least keep an open mind?" Kimberly asked, pacing the room.

"Okay, for you," she said, hoping to end the conversation. Will you grab the small suitcase from the third cupboard?"

Kimberly placed the case on the bed and unzipped it. "What can I do to help?"

"Sit and relax." Jennifer gathered her things and placed them in the case. "Perhaps tomorrow I can make an appointment to have my hair washed. There's still some dried blood in it."

Kimberly settled in on the navy-blue fainting couch. "I'll call the salon in the morning."

"Thanks."

Downstairs, they found Jacks, drink in hand, looking at pictures on the mantel.

"We're finally back. Sorry it took so long," Jennifer said, placing the suitcase on the sofa.

"No problem. You have a beautiful home. I gather these are your daughters." He lifted a silver picture frame.

"Yes. That was taken at the last soccer game of the season."

Jacks returned the frame to the polished oak surface. "They're certainly cute."

"They're my pride and joy," Jennifer said as she closed the blinds on the picture window.

He sipped his drink before asking, "Who plays the baby grand?"

"We all do. Nothing else would quite work in front

of the picture window. Do you play?"

"Three years of lessons to please Mom, I'm very rusty. Where do your girls go to school?"

Kimberly joined the conversation. "Okay, you two, it's time to go. Our patient needs to rest."

"She'd make a wonderful nag of a mother," Jennifer said with a chuckle.

"You're looking a bit pale," Jacks said before he walked into the kitchen, rinsed his glass, found the dishwasher, and placed the glass inside.

"Thanks for all your help today," Jennifer said when he returned.

"I call them like I see them. You'll always get the truth from me."

Jennifer heard the shift in his tone, the look on his face gave her the impression he hadn't meant to be so serious. She touched his arm, "Somehow, I knew that. The question is can you tango?"

His relaxed smile met hers. "Actually, I can."

"Perhaps I'll let you give me a spin," Jennifer paused, "on the dance floor, that is," she added with a wink and headed toward the door. The thought of being in his arms made her forget the headache as her mind went straight to Jacks' hands on her body. Good Lord, she was in big trouble. What was it about this guy?

****

Brandon was waiting at the street and directed his wife into the garage. "It appears the party carried on fine without us," Kimberly said.

"How are you, sweetie?" Brandon asked as he opened the door and took Jennifer's hand.

"I'm fine, fifteen stitches and one heck of a headache, but the worst part, no scotch."

"Must have a concussion?" he replied, taking the bag of medicine and medical supplies from her.

"Yep. I need to take it easy for a couple of days."

"You're staying here, right?"

Jennifer responded as the group headed in the front door. "Of course, your wife wouldn't have it any other way."

"I'll carry your bag upstairs if you like," Jacks said.

"Top of the stairs and straight ahead," Kimberly added.

"Jacks, thanks," Jennifer said as he started up the stairs. She quickly added, "Thanks for everything today."

"No problem, I'll be right back," Jacks said before taking the stairs two at a time.

Jennifer paused in the kitchen to trim the rose and place it in the small bud vase. Despite the pain, she allowed her mind to drift. Would his kisses send spirals of excitement through her body? Would it be strange to kiss someone other than her ex? What were these flames of desire he'd fanned in her? If they had a relationship, would he grow tired of her, too?

****

Jacks stood on the porch watching Jennifer sip her drink. He'd seen the rose in the yellow crystal vase as he walked through the kitchen. What was it about this woman? It was those lavender eyes he saw when he tried to fall asleep. This was insane.

"Come on, let's join the party," Brandon said.

"I need to get a beer first," Jacks said.

Brandon chuckled. "The wash tub's right beside you."

"So, it is." Jacks selected a bottle, removed the top,

47

and took a long draw.

"I know that look. She's got your interest?" Brandon said.

"Who?" Jacks said, sitting on the settee.

"Okay, Romeo, keep lying to yourself. Jennifer's amazing. We've been friends since my Dorothy died." Brandon paused and took a sip of his drink. "She was married to a real piece of work, the male version of your ex."

"Wow, I wouldn't wish that on anybody, and yes, she has my attention."

"Go talk to her," Brandon said, placing his left hand on the young man's shoulder and nudging him along.

"Thanks, Dad," Jacks said, stood, and stepped down the stairs. How had she gotten through the wall of defenses he built over the last two years? If he took a chance, would she leave him too? Trash his life and walk away? No. Not Jennifer. She might trash his heart but not his life. Somehow in his gut, he knew that was true.

****

Jennifer noticed Jacks the minute he stepped on the deck, there was that tingle again, and the breeze was far from cool.

Kimberly leaned in and spoke in a low tone. "Here he comes, pilot on final approach."

"Stop that." Jennifer swatted her friend's hand.

"Ladies, can I get either of you anything?"

"Jacks, take my seat. It's time for me to check on dinner." She turned to Jennifer. "Sweetie, you want more tea?"

"No, I'm okay," she said, shaking her head.

"How are you feeling?" Jacks asked as he sat in the chair Kimberly vacated.

"Good as can be expected, I guess. I still feel rather foolish about the whole thing," she said before sipping her tea.

"Are you kidding? You were the main entertainment, didn't Kimberly tell you? She was going to sell tickets, but I convinced her it was over the top, even for one of her parties."

Jennifer smiled and asked. "So, you've heard about her parties?"

"Hasn't everyone in Hampton Roads?" He took a sip of his beer and placed it in the holder on the arm of the chair. "I suggest our next date be a bit less dramatic, something between grocery shopping and an activity that leads to stitches."

Was he asking her out? "Perhaps," she responded, playing with her ponytail.

"Noncommittal, I like that, presents a challenge." He leaned back in the chair and took a slow drink of his beer.

"Keep trying. I'm sure you haven't even skimmed the surface of your storehouse of pickup lines," Jennifer said.

"Would that be a dare?"

"Just a statement. I'm going inside out of the sun for a while. See you later, good-looking."

"How about a goodbye kiss, sweetheart?"

Jennifer leaned down, grinned, and moved her lips toward his. At the last second, she stopped and kissed him on the forehead. "I never kiss until—let me see—the sixth date."

****

As she walked away, Jacks admired the gentle sway of her heart-shaped ass. He let his head fall back in the chair and closed his eyes. Was it his imagination, or had her eyes darkened to deep purple? He could go after her and find out, but unfortunately, walking anywhere right now wouldn't be a good thing. Jennifer had his libido churning, and it was very apparent how much.

He'd have to sit and think about anything to reduce the tightness in his shorts, and he knew just what would do the trick, his ex-wife. He envisioned her yelling the reason she slept with other men was because he was a shitty, unimaginative lover. Yep, that did the trick.

Chapter Five

Jennifer hugged her best friend. "I had a great time. Thanks for inviting me."

"The girls won't be home until tomorrow. You could stay another night. We'd love the company," Kimberly said, holding her friend at arm's length.

Brandon smiled and winked. "Some more than others."

Jennifer smiled and felt the blush creep to her cheeks. "I've a dozen things to do. Plus, you have a house full with Jacks and Mike staying here until they find a place. Thanks for the offer. I'm feeling fine."

"I'll carry your bag," Jacks said.

"Thanks." Jennifer hugged Kimberly again.

Jacks and Jennifer walked in silence to her car. She opened the hatch, and Jacks set the overnight case inside. He ran his fingers down Jennifer's arm as she closed it.

"How about lunch next week?" Jacks asked.

"Sure." She removed a pen and business card from her purse, turned it over, and printed her cell phone number. You can reach me at either of these numbers."

"I finally get your phone number, and it only took what, eighteen months? I knew persistence would pay off," he joked, took the card, and let his thumb linger on her palm.

Her skin tingled at his touch, her throat was dry, and she wasn't sure what to say.

Jacks didn't skip a beat and continued. "It was nice seeing you again." His voice had taken on a low and seductive tone.

"Thanks for coming to my rescue. I'm glad the blood washed out of your shirt." Jennifer touched her stitches.

"No problem." Jacks slid his hand from hers. "I'll talk to you soon."

"I'll look forward to it." *Why did he make her feel like an awkward teenager?*

****

She was turning into her driveway when her cell phone rang. "This is Dr. Ryan."

"Well, hello, Dr. Ryan. This is Commander Williams."

"Hey," she said and felt a grin grow.

"Would you like to have lunch tomorrow?"

"Sure. I'll be at Norfolk Naval, will noon at the Officer's Club work?" *Do I sound desperate?*

"See you there."

She smiled. It was wonderful to have a man make a fuss. He seemed nice, but things with Phillip began wonderfully and then went to hell. It's a good thing Jacks was deploying soon. There wouldn't be time for an entanglement. It would be fun to spend time with a man. A wave of anxiety rolled over her. What happened if he wanted to have sex? She could always say no, or yes if the mood hit. *First things first Jennifer, its lunch, not a marriage proposal.* She closed her eyes and enjoyed the vision of Jacks playing volleyball.

****

Jacks leaned against the railing and watched Jennifer cross the parking lot. Desire to kiss her crawled up from the depths of his soul. What was it about this woman? She made him nervous as hell. He fought to control his breathing as she approached. "Hello." Jennifer smiled, which didn't help the battle to regain his composure.

"Hey, how are you?" Jennifer asked.

"Wonderful, now that you're here." *That's it, go for humor.*

She rolled her eyes and chuckled. "Are you always such an outlandish flirt?"

"It only seems to come out when I'm around you."

"Plus, you've got to keep up your cocky pilot façade." Jennifer smiled and winked.

Jacks touched his palm to his chest and said, "You've wounded my heart, again."

She pulled his hand from his chest. "Come on, let's have lunch."

They walked hand in hand to the entrance, Jacks opened the door. "Good afternoon, two for lunch?" the hostess asked.

Jacks answered, "Yes. May we have a table overlooking the water?"

"Right this way."

He guided Jennifer with his hand in the small of her back. The contact and her scent caused a sensual jolt to his system. Today, she smelled of coconuts.

"Will this do, sir?" the hostess asked, pointing to a table overlooking the bay.

"Perfect," Jacks said, pulling out Jennifer's chair.

The hostess placed the menus on the table. "Your waitress will be right with you."

"Great," Jacks replied.

"The view's amazing," Jennifer said, focusing on

the shoreline.

"Yes, it is." His gaze met hers when she turned.

"Stop that."

Jacks smiled at the blush that crept on her face. "Okay, for now. What do you do for fun?" *Change the subject before you say something stupid.*

"Well, let me see, I love to bike."

"Motor or peddle?" he inquired.

"Excuse me, I'm Monica. I'll be your waitress. Would you like to hear the specials?"

"Sure," Jacks answered.

"We have two. Honey crusted salmon with fresh steamed vegetables or a buffalo burger with bacon and your choice of cheese, comes with fries."

Jacks smiled at his lunch companion. "What would you like?"

Jennifer grinned before answering. "No choice, the burger medium rare, provolone cheese, fries crispy, and iced tea."

"Woman after my own heart, same for me," Jacks said and handed Monica the menus.

"It'll be right out."

"Thanks. Where were we? Oh, yes. Do you like bicycles or motorcycles?" Jacks asked again.

"Bicycle, I've never been on a motorcycle."

Jacks felt the tightness in his pants as he slid his hand over hers and whispered, "You, my dear, have lived a sheltered life. Perhaps you'll allow me the pleasure of giving you your first ride." After a short pause, he continued, "On my bike, that is."

The waitress placed two glasses of tea on the table.

"Thanks," he said, never breaking eye contact with Jennifer.

"I'd love to, but I don't have a helmet or anything," she said, stroking his hand with her fingers.

"I have gear you can use," Jacks said quickly.

Jennifer sipped her drink and grinned at him over her glass. "How many other women have used your gear, Commander Williams?"

His response came with a wide smile. "Are we still talking motorcycles?"

"Of course, that's the topic at hand."

"Now who's being the flirt?" Jacks winked and sipped his drink before he continued. "There's a ride at the end of next month, starts Friday and ends Monday. Brandon and Kimberly are going, and my brothers will probably take part, too." Jacks really wanted her to join him.

"Sounds like something I'd like to try."

"Good. It's a fund raiser for therapy dogs for wounded troops. The best part is it includes riding the Tail of the Dragon, three hundred eighteen curves in eleven miles. Survive, and you have bragging rights."

Jennifer's eyes were round, she nodded, but her expression wasn't that of someone fully convinced.

"You'd have to hold tight and mold your body to mine to ensure we make the curves safely." His fingers continued to play with hers. *He never talks this much to anyone. What's up?*

"I could do that." She accented her comment with a wink. "Hotels or tents for the overnights?"

"Which would you prefer?"

"Hotel, I think. I reserve my camping for scouting, plus I tend to attract rain."

"Hotels it is. We'll need to take a few short rides before you try a long one. You up for that?"

She leaned forward. "I think I'd like to take a ride with you, Jacks Williams. Can you teach me what I need to know so you can enjoy the ride and not worry about me?"

"Oh yeah," he said with a grin. "Put yourself in my hands." The thought of Jennifer on his bike quickly shifted to her in his bed. He was glad lunch arrived before his mind got him into trouble.

****

Jacks felt like a schoolboy taking a girl out for the first time. They'd planned a dinner for the next weekend when her daughters were visiting their father. Here he was standing at her door holding two dozen yellow roses, scared silly. He closed his eyes and took a deep breath before knocking. *Why the hell was he so nervous?*

"Hey," Jennifer said, opening the door.

Her smile was amazing. "These are for you." He handed her the bouquet.

"How did you know yellow roses are my favorite? They're beautiful, thank you." She stood on her tiptoes and brushed her lips over his cheek. "Come on in."

"I did a bit of recon," Jacks said.

"You asked Kimberly," Jennifer said as she closed the door.

"A Navy aviator never reveals his source," he advised adding a wink.

Her smile made him grin.

Her tempting mouth curved as she laughed. "Would you like a glass of wine before we head out?" Jennifer asked.

"Absolutely."

"I guess you remember the kitchen is right this way," she said and headed down the short hallway.

Jacks followed her and enjoyed the view of her round butt in the exquisitely tailored navy pants.

"You can hang your coat on any of the hooks," she said and pointed to the rack over a polished wooden church pew.

"Cool coat rack. Are the hooks doorknobs?"

"Yep, antiques. I collected for years. Not really sure what I'd do with them, and then I saw the idea online. Which do you prefer, red or white wine?" she asked as she removed a vase from the cabinet and placed it on the island.

"White works," he answered on automatic as he took in the room. "I didn't see much of the room when I was here the other day." A huge fireplace covered almost the entire back wall of the room. "The fireplace is amazing. Is it original?"

"Yep, this was the original summer kitchen built in 1846. I love the stonework on the chimney. One of the general contractors I interviewed to handle the remodel said it would be cheaper to pull it down and put in a new one. He didn't get the job."

"Great choice."

She retrieved a bottle from the chiller. "This is an Australian Sauvignon Blanc Kimberly and Brandon gave me as a housewarming present." She grabbed two glasses and a corkscrew and placed them on the counter. "Do you mind opening the bottle while I arrange the flowers?"

"No problem. You have a beautiful home," he said and removed the foil from the bottle.

"After the divorce, the girls and I wanted to start with a clean slate. A new house seemed like the right place to begin."

"I understand. After my divorce, I requested a transfer. I needed to start over. The United States Navy was happy to comply. I was stationed in Pensacola, Florida."

"Kimberly was stationed there for a while. I visited her. It seemed like a nice assignment," Jennifer said and cut the greenery.

"It seemed to work for me." Jacks opened the wine and poured each half a glass. "Here you go."

"Cheers," she said and touched her glass to his. She took a sip and returned to trimming the stems of the roses.

Jacks leaned against the counter and watched. "You're a florist, too? The arrangement's beautiful."

"Not really, simply a well-prepared scout. Growing up, I lived with my aunt in Tallahassee. She loved plants and had amazing gardens. Hosting afternoon teas and garden parties were her favorite things. I loved to help make centerpieces."

"You speak of her in the past tense. I gather she's deceased."

"Four years ago, she donated her house and gardens to the local garden club."

"That was a generous thing to do," he said.

"She was a special woman."

As the smile slipped from her lips, Jacks shifted the conversation. He lifted the wine glass and said, "Wine glasses engraved with dachshunds; should I prepare for the attack of the hounds?"

"Not right now. My daughters would love to have one each." She sipped her wine before continuing. "I'm trying to delay the inevitable."

"Sounds like there's a story there," Jacks said,

leaning against the marble countertop.

"I'll save it for another time."

"Okay, I'll hold you to that. This wine has a great flavor. Are you a wine snob?"

Her laugh was amazing, made him smile. "I'm getting there. The wine chiller came with the house. I've always enjoyed wine. I usually drank what my ex-husband selected; I'm learning he didn't have very good taste." She shrugged her shoulders.

He took a sip of wine and said, "My ex-wife's idea of good wine was anything with an easy open cap. She wasn't smart enough to operate a corkscrew."

"Sounds like both our marriages were an adventure." Jennifer slipped three roses into the vase.

"You wouldn't believe me if I told you," he said before sipping his wine.

"Done." Jennifer slid the vase to the center of the island. "Would you like to watch the sunset while we finish our wine?"

"Sure." He took the hand she offered.

"Best seats in the house are this way." She led him to the sunroom.

Jacks took in the space; the room was decorated in a nautical theme. A sitting area with sectional sofas and wicker tables faced the bank of six floor-to-ceiling windows. Different shaped pillows with sea life, coral, floral, and anchor patterns were placed around the furniture. The hues of blues and greens gave the space a welcome feel.

The same theme was carried over to the white wicker dining set with tropical design cushions. The Florida room was full of budding multicolored flowers and ferns. Candles of various sizes burned around the room; the smell was familiar—an Italian seaside garden. He smiled, recalling his time on leave in Italy. The space suited her and would make any visitor welcome.

"Have a seat." She pointed to the sofa. "The girls and I eat dinner here most nights. It's my favorite part of the house," Jennifer said and joined him.

"I can see why. The view's amazing, the leaves changing colors and the ducks on the water set a beautiful scene. A quiet place to reflect."

"Or curl up and read a book?"

"The water is smooth as glass today. Do you have a boat?"

"Not yet. The previous owners left two kayaks. The girls keep dropping hints about jet skis for their birthday. I don't think I'm ready for that," she said, shaking her head.

Jacks read the mild panic that bubbled in her voice and shone in her eyes. "How old will they be?"

"Fifteen." Jennifer placed her wine glass on the table.

"They're reaching the milestone of learning to drive."

Jennifer waved her hands in the air. "Don't remind me. It'll be nice when they can drive themselves to school and activities. Thankfully, that's still a year away. I signed them up for driver's training next summer. It saves me the heart attack and puts them off for a while."

"I can't imagine going through that. My dad taught me, and I still recall the fear in his eyes."

"It's funny. I remember thinking they'd never be old enough to potty-train, much less go to school. Now they're talking about colleges. I'm not sure where the time went."

"Everyone I know who has kids says the same thing." Jacks swirled the liquid in his glass. "This is an exceptional wine."

"Thanks. Do you have children?" Jennifer asked and took a sip from her glass.

"No. I never felt like the time was right which turned out to be the best decision. Donna, my ex, would have used a child as a pawn or a weapon to her advantage. You and your ex seem to get along."

"Only because I understand how important it is for the girls. It hasn't been easy. We divorced because his girlfriend was pregnant."

"Ouch, which had to hurt." He turned slightly to face her and took her hand.

"Phillip didn't comprehend dating stops when you get married. I guess it could've been worse. He could have run away with the circus," she said with a laugh.

"That's certainly looking at the glass half full."

"I guess." She shrugged her shoulders.

"How long were you married?" Jacks asked.

"A bit over twenty years. How about you?"

"Eight. She didn't care for the military—that's not exactly true. She loved military men, and lots of them, just not me."

"Wow. Sorry, I know how that feels."

"Time heals a great deal of wounds."

"Yes, it does. Do you have brothers and sisters?"

"Two brothers, Alex and Max. I generally call them by their given names, Alexander and Maxwell, to get on their nerves."

"What do they call you to get on your nerves?"

"My middle name."

Jennifer sipped her wine and asked, "So what's your

middle name?"

"We won't discuss that until our eighth date or so."

She let out a giggle. "I see. Are all of you in the military?"

"No. Alex and I went into what the three of us call the family business. Max is a journalist."

"The Navy's the family business?" Jennifer asked.

"Yes. When you meet my father, you'll hear how six generations have served in the military. The last four, well, five with me, were Navy. My grandfather enlisted, my father's Admiral Williams." The fact he wanted her to meet his family rattled his inner calm.

Jennifer sat forward. "*The* Admiral Williams, as in Commander of the Pacific theater, Joint Chief of Staff, and advisor to the President, Admiral Williams?" Her mouth dropped open, her tone filled with awe and respect.

"Guilty as charged," he said as his face split into a wide grin.

"That means your mother's Martha Williams. She writes wonderful children's books about Coco the monkey, two dachshunds, and three little boys. And she's—wait, I know—a pediatric surgeon."

He heard the excitement in her voice. "She'd be thrilled you mentioned her books first. She's been retired from the medical profession for about three years, and writing is her one true passion. You obviously know her work?"

"Are you kidding? Morgan and Madison learned to read with her books. I was able to squash the monkey request, but that's why they're still after me for dachshund puppies." After a pause, she grinned. "Jacks, Alex, and Max. You were the boys that found Coco the spider monkey?"

"Guilty again."

"So there really was a Coco?" She leaned in close and asked in a low tone as if she knew she was asking for insider information but couldn't help herself.

"Sorry, I can neither confirm nor deny."

She set her glass on the coffee table. Stood, held out her hand. "Come on, I want to show you something upstairs."

"Your bedroom? This is a first; Coco never got me into a lady's bed."

She laughed. "Stop it. Come on."

Jacks followed Jennifer upstairs. "In here, my girls have autographed pictures of your mom with them hanging over there." She pointed to the oak frames on the wall over the girls' beds. "We met your mom in Atlanta eight years ago, at a book signing and lunch."

"She loves those events." He leaned in and whispered. "If you mention I told you this, I'll deny it. She's releasing a new series for teenagers. The first one is set to release in January."

"I promise, not a word." She placed an imaginary X over her heart. Will you let me know when I can pre-order? The girls will love a new series."

He turned to face her, stepped closer, and smiled. "I think I can make that happen. While we're here, can I see your bedroom?"

She winked and replied, "Maybe a peek. It's this way." At the end of the hall, she opened one of two carved wooden doors and stepped inside. "I turned two rooms into a master suite and added a balcony." As she spoke, Jennifer opened one of the two sets of French doors to the veranda. "Check out the view from here."

Chapter Six

Jacks focused on the king-size cherry oak bed. A delicate white lace canopy with scalloped edges draped to meet matching linen curtains, each tied with navy blue silk ribbons to the four posts. Pillows of assorted sizes, shapes, and shades of blue accented the simple white comforter.

He quickly scanned the room. Her dressing table matched the polished bed. Arranged on top were cobalt glass bottles. A silver brush and comb set rested on a matching tray. Jennifer Ryan might be a military officer on the outside, but in here, she was one hundred percent woman.

He followed Jennifer out the French doors onto the balcony. He took in the yard. Evergreens and other flowers native to the state were arranged in multicolor beds along the walkways. The breeze surrounded him with a woodsy, sweet aroma that brought about memories of planting roses with his mother. The remembering brought on an inner peace.

"Is that a pelican?" Jacks asked, trying to put the memory away for later.

"Yes. We see them from time to time. Being on Chesapeake Bay all sorts of wildlife pay us a visit. I'm constantly putting out corn and bird seed. It continues to disappear, so something's enjoying it," Jennifer said.

"I can see why you fell in love with this place."

64

Jennifer led him to the swing. "I wanted to give the girls a home they could always come back to. A place that would always be home. I missed that growing up. I don't remember a time my parents weren't divorced. I spent a week with each one. Back and forth like a ping pong ball."

"That had to be difficult."

"Not too bad. From what I recall, they got along well. Had to, I guess. They were joint owners in an import/export business. They were on a business trip when my dad's plane crashed. I was twelve. That's when I went to live with my Aunt Lois."

"Wow. I can't imagine that kind of loss. Did you two get along?" Jacks slipped his arm around Jennifer's shoulder. He pushed against the floor with his left foot, and the swing moved smoothly back and forth.

"Very much so, but I didn't make it easy on her, at least not at first. I was mad at the world and acted out. Lois sent me to see a psychologist, Dr. Simmons. She helped me so much. With her guidance, I learned to work through my pain and anger. That's why I decided to become a psychologist. What about you? What was it like being a Navy kid?"

"Outstanding, we lived all over the world. I can't imagine what it is like living in the same place all my life. My parents retired to Cambridge, Massachusetts three years ago." As they spoke, he ran his fingers across her knuckles.

"Why did you become a pilot?" Jennifer asked as she shifted a bit closer.

"I was a SEAL, and the chance presented itself. I did it," he replied with a shrug.

"Okay, why did you become a SEAL?"

"Blow shit up, of course," he answered quickly. "Sorry. Shoot big guns. You know, every little boy's fantasies."

"No problem. I've heard that word before. Why put yourself through that?"

"It was a dare, so I did it."

"That's right, you like a good dare."

She responded with a smile that caused his sexual temperature to rise. "Be careful what challenges you throw my way. I've never let one by yet."

"Is that a warning not to dare you? Or a promise you'll take any I issue?"

"I guess you have to wait and see," Jacks said. He pulled her hand to his lips and kissed it. "This is very nice, so peaceful. I could spend hours relaxing here."

"I know." She turned her hand over and interlaced her fingers with his.

His heart pounded. The touch of her hand sent tingles surging through his body. They sat in silence and Jacks felt an inner peace roll over him.

Jennifer broke the silence. "Shall we head out to dinner?"

"Absolutely." Jacks stood and offered his hand. She took it and slowly rose. He stepped in close and lifted her chin. Gently brushed his lips against hers and whispered. "Now our first kiss is out of the way. We can enjoy dinner and relax." The warmth of her breath caused his heart to race.

Jack's whole being filled with a wanting to know everything about Jennifer; he needed to get his emotions in check. Somewhere in the back of his mind, a voice whispered, *Keep kidding yourself; your life will never be the same.*

66

****

Jennifer settled in at the table. "This will be fun. I haven't had fondue in years."

"I like the fact it's a slow process. You can take all the time you need and enjoy yourself."

Jennifer grinned. "Why do I get the idea you like taking your time on things?"

"I guess I do. My father taught me when you do things slow and steady, it allows for the full enjoyment of the project." Jacks stroked his fingertips over her hand.

Before Jennifer could respond, the waiter appeared.

"Good evening. My name is Nathan, and I'll be your server tonight," he supplied and placed menus on the table in front of Jacks and Jennifer. "Have you been to our restaurant before?"

Both Jennifer and Jacks spoke at the same time. "Yes."

"Very good. Would you like to start with something to drink?"

Jacks took a quick peruse of the wine list and asked, "Jennifer, what about we continue with the sauvignon blanc?"

"I'd like water as well."

"Nathan, a bottle of the house white wine and two waters, please."

"Very good, sir," the waiter replied. "Will you be enjoying the four courses experience this evening?"

"Yes," Jacks said and placed his hand on Jennifer's.

"Very good. The first course is the cheese appetizer. You will find the selections on page two of the menu. I'll retrieve your wine while you decide on your cheese."

"Thank you," Jennifer said and opened the menu.

After a few seconds, she asked, "See anything thing you like?"

When her eyes met Jacks', he winked and said, "Oh yeah, very much."

The heat crept from her toes to her scalp. "I meant from the menu."

"Oh, let me see, how about the Classic Alpine?"

"Here you are," Nathan said, pouring a small amount of the wine into a glass and offering it to Jacks.

Jennifer wondered what the wine would taste like on Jacks lips as he sipped the wine. He looked so at home and relaxed. Phillip had played the part well, but it was all for show. Could Jacks be like her ex? How would she ever be sure again about anyone she dated?"

Jacks touched Jennifer's hand. "You look so serious. Everything okay?"

"Yes. Just thinking, that's all."

"Anything you want to share?"

"No. Yes. I'm not sure," Jennifer stammered.

"I'm here if you need an ear." He held both hands up. "This is a no-judgment zone."

"Thanks, that means a great deal."

"Try the wine. It's surprisingly good."

****

Jacks didn't want the night to end. New, uncomfortable emotions surrounded him. At the same time, there was a contentment of sorts. "Would you like to go for a walk on the beach?" he suggested as an afterthought.

"Sounds like a wonderful idea," Jennifer said in a silky voice.

They headed down Twenty-First Street to the boardwalk. "Thank you for dinner—it was wonderful.

The girls love fondue, but for some reason we never think to come here."

At the water's edge they removed their shoes. The breeze was crisp but energizing. He reached for her hand. To his delight, she took it without hesitation.

"You really up for the bike fund raiser?" Jacks asked.

"Yep. I talked to Kimberly about it. It sounds like fun."

"My housemates and their wives are taking part. I'm not sure if they're riding in cages or on bikes."

"Cages?" Jennifer stopped and turned quickly to stare at him.

He could only describe the look on her face as fear instead of confusion. Jacks laughed, smiling at her expression and the tone in her voice. "Sorry. If you drive or ride in a support car, it's considered the safety cage. You're surrounded with the safety of the car. The look on your face was classic."

"You caught me by surprise, nothing you hear often. Guess I have a great deal to learn."

"I'm ready and willing to teach you." Jacks said, accenting his comment with a wink and smile. He pulled Jennifer into his arms. Trying to keep her off balance, he teased her lips with his ever so briefly with light kisses before continuing the conversation. "How did you and Kimberly meet?"

"Officer's Candidate School, we corresponded for years. Then boom, here she was in Hampton Roads."

"I understand you introduced her to Brandon."

"One of my finer moments," she responded with a grin. "You should have seen them. There were fireworks going off. Less than a year later, they were married."

Jennifer looked at her watch. "Is it really one thirty?"

Jacks instinctively looked at his watch. "Yes. Is that a problem? You gonna turn into a pumpkin?"

"No," she said and laughed. "I'm usually heading to bed by nine. But I'm not the least bit tired. The twins have a soccer game in the morning at eight thirty. I said I'd be there at kick-off."

"I need to get you home."

"Probably a clever idea."

Settled in the car, Jacks took her hand, pulled it to his lips, and placed a small kiss on the back of her hand. Their fingers stayed intertwined until he parked in Jennifer's driveway.

He turned to face her. "I had a wonderful time."

"Me too; thanks again for dinner."

"It was my pleasure. You make me smile. It's been a long time since I've done that, for real anyway."

"I understand. Sometimes it's easier to pretend to be happy, so people leave you alone."

"That's for sure."

Jacks exited his side of the vehicle, walked around, and opened the passenger door. He took her hand as she stepped onto the running board and didn't let go as they walked toward the front porch.

In the soft glow of the blue porch light, he looked down into her eyes. "You know I'll be deploying soon. I understand this isn't conducive to starting a relationship. But I'd like to spend time with you until I leave."

"I'd like that very much. The past year has been an emotional roller coaster. My daughters have been my focus. Why don't we take this one day at a time?"

"Works for me," he said. "Would you like to do something tomorrow after the soccer game?"

Her smile answered him long before the words. "A nor'easter is supposed to move in tomorrow. We'll need to do something indoors."

Jacks couldn't mask his smile. He brushed her cheek with his fingertips. "What, pray tell, do you have in mind?" he asked as he quirked an eyebrow.

Even in the low light, he could see the color rise in her cheeks. "No. I meant we needed to do something inside. I wasn't trying to seduce you."

"Wow. I think my manhood's been wounded, again. You're making a habit of that." Confusion danced in Jennifer's eyes as he continued. "So. you were trying to seduce me? Now we're getting someplace. Let me kiss you. Save you from further damaging my ego."

There was a tingling in the pit of his stomach. His arms encircled her, one hand in the small of her back, the other at the nape of her neck. He drew her body closer. Her uneven breath drifted against his cheek. The touch, the scent of her, drew him like a magnet. He wanted to photograph her with his eyes. Remember everything, the dusky rose of her cheeks and the tempting curve of her mouth.

The fall breeze danced around them, and she shivered against him. Was it excitement? She ran her hands around his neck and molded her body to his. His mouth covered hers with a hunger that contradicted his outward calm. Her lips parted, and he tasted and took. Her tongue sent shivers of desire pulsing through him.

Her response drove him. He stroked her hair. Shifted and kissed her again. Reclaiming her lips, he pulled her tight against him. Raising his mouth from hers, he gazed into her eyes. He wanted to pull her inside and make love with her. Instead, he brushed his tongue over her swollen lips. Kissed her nose.

Her lavender eyes had darkened to amethyst and sparkled in the moonlight. He watched her chest rise and fall. More, he needed more. Her flavor had become a drug—one he'd crave for the rest of his life.

"How about we try dinner and a movie?" he asked.

"What?" she muttered hastily.

"Tomorrow afternoon. Let's do dinner and a movie?"

"Okay. Call me," Jennifer said as she dropped her keys, picked them up, and dropped them again.

"Let me do that for you." He took the keys, unlocked and opened the door. She didn't move. "Are you okay?"

"Yes. I guess." Her tone was so sweet and tender.

"What's wrong?"

"I've never been kissed by anyone but my ex. It was different."

Jacks grinned and ran his hand down her cheek. "Good different, I hope."

"Oh yes. I thought it'd be weird the first time."

"Should I kiss you again?" he asked, stepping close, caressing her collar bone with his fingertips.

"No," she replied quickly and a bit too loud.

Her quick response made him grin and chuckle before he spoke. "No, never, or not right now?"

"Later, not now."

He kissed her on the forehead. "I'll call you around two o'clock. We'll make a plan." He waited until she closed and bolted the door. He whistled as he turned and headed toward his car. Tossed his keys in the air and caught them. *This is going to be an adventure for so many reasons.*

Jacks' mind was focused on the night and the amazing kiss; he didn't notice the truck parked down the block from Jennifer's house.

Chapter Seven

Jennifer sipped her morning coffee and dialed her best friend.

"Hey there, how was last night?" Kimberly's cheerful voice asked without waiting for a response.

Jennifer couldn't suppress the giggle before she spoke. "I acted like a fickle schoolgirl. Rattled on like a fool who'd never been kissed; he must think I'm a complete idiot."

"Was the kiss really wonderful, or compared to Phillip, it was good?"

Jennifer leaned on the kitchen island. "There's no comparison. He made my head swim, could've taken me right there on the front porch." She felt the heat rising on her cheeks again.

"Wow. Now that's a kiss." Kimberly's enthusiasm danced through the phone with each word.

Jennifer played with her coffee cup. "Maybe since it's been so long, I lost my bearings."

"The question is, what are you going to do about it?"

"Hell, if I know. Right now, I want to take him to bed and never get out. All he did was kiss me and touch my face. I took off like a roman candle." Jennifer paced around the kitchen.

"My advice, jump him this afternoon. You're both adults. What's the downside?"

"Thanks. I'll keep your suggestion in mind."

"Okay, you two come for dinner. We'll watch a movie or play cards. I'll protect you from yourself. Brandon can line up buckets of cold water in case the two of you spontaneously combust."

Jennifer felt a warm glow flow through her. "I'll talk to you later."

Kimberly managed to get one more laugh and comment in. "Take him to bed. You need it.'"

"Bye." *Take him to bed? Maybe she would.*

****

A major storm was raging when Jacks arrived for dinner. The opened garage was a welcome greeting.

Jennifer stepped into view, and he couldn't take his eyes off her. She was stunning in jeans, a copper blouse, and a blue and copper button-up sweater. He took in the sight of her. Her long curls were captured in a bun. "Hello, beautiful."

"Hey. Come inside. I have a fire going in the kitchen." She waved him toward the door. "The storm roared in with cold temperatures."

"Best offer I've had in a long time," he said and swept her weightlessly into his arms. Her lips were warm and sweet. She tasted of fresh peppermint. With regret, he allowed her to slide down his body.

"Come on in." She took his hand and led him into the kitchen.

The last time he visited, he hadn't noticed the exposed brick wall. Like last night, the fire provided welcomed warmth.

Jacks leaned against the island and enjoyed the view of her butt as she ladled cider into two mugs. He imagined what type of panties she wore, thong, bikini, lacey, or simple plain ones. That was one of a dozen

75

things he wanted to know. Questions that were driving him crazy.

"Was the weather bad for your drive?" she asked and placed the mug on the marble-topped island.

"No, not at all. Something smells wonderful."

"There were fresh lobsters at the market this morning. I made lobster stew and bread."

Jacks lifted his cup. "I may be in love."

She raised her cup in a toast. "Don't get carried away, sailor. Phillip really made me angry at the soccer game. Baking bread allows me to release my frustration. Kneading dough takes a great deal of effort."

"So, if the man in your life comes home to the sweet smell of homemade bread, it's not a good thing?"

"Depends. Sometimes it is, others it's not. He has to figure it out." The grin and sparkle in her eyes made him smile.

"I gather today, for me, it's a good thing. All your aggression is gone?" he asked, stepping toward her.

"Absolutely."

"Good." He placed his mug on the counter, reached for her hands, and she stepped into his arms. He raised her chin slightly with his thumb. She stood on her tiptoes, and ran her arms around his waist and up his back.

His lips drank from hers as if she offered a rare wine. The smells of the kitchen and her scent blended to form an exotic mixture. The kiss continued until a moan escaped her throat. Slowly he released her and reveled in the fact her eyes were pools of deep purple. Every time his gaze met hers, his heart thundered.

*****

Jennifer drifted on a cloud. She mentally shook her head before speaking. "Shall we head to the porch before the cider gets cold?"

"Sounds good," Jacks said, picked up his mug, and followed Jennifer through the brick archway.

She paused at the first window as lightning tore across the sky. When she jumped at the thunder, Jacks slid his arm around her waist. A peaceful sensation she'd never experienced filled her heart. "I love to watch the weather."

"One of my favorite things, too. It's magical." Whitecaps of the Chesapeake Bay splashed against the dock; wind whipped water across the wooden walkway. The brass lantern chandelier in the gazebo swung back and forth in the fierce wind and driving rain.

"I'm glad I put the furniture in the boat house. It would probably be in the bay by now," Jennifer said, leading Jacks to the sofa.

"Do you use the outdoor kitchen?" Jacks asked after he sipped his cider.

"Pretty often. The girls and their friends practically lived outside all summer. Swimming, kayaking, and hanging out. I like the fact their friends come here. I know what they're doing."

Jacks turned toward her. "Wherever we were stationed growing up, our house was the gathering place. I thought it was cool and my parents liked it. I didn't understand their ulterior motive. Do you swim or kayak?"

"I love to swim. Kayaking's another story. I haven't gotten the opportunity. It's hard to get a turn with the kids using them. What about you?"

"Scuba diving or snorkeling are my favorite water activities." He winked and added a smile. "There's another one I enjoy more, but the situation hasn't presented itself in a while."

"Really, and what would that be?"

"Get your mind out of the gutter, Colonel." He caressed her hand with his thumb. "I love fishing."

Tingles crept up her arm, and a wave washed over her. Jennifer rolled her eyes and said, "You are such a flirt."

"Guess I am." He brushed his fingers down her cheek. Resting her chin between his thumb and forefinger, he gently nudged her face toward his. Locking eyes, he moved his mouth over hers, gently claiming her lips.

His lips were like the sweet whisper of a promise, a delicious sensation. The intimacy of the moment swirled around her, clouded her brain. She was falling into a pit of raw desire. She fought to slow her out-of-control breathing.

Slowly he retreated and whispered, "Baby, the smell of the fresh bread is driving me crazy. Suddenly I'm starving."

His quick switch surprised her. "What?" she somehow managed to ask.

"Lunch. Are you ready for lunch?"

She drew in a long, deep breath. "We can eat in the kitchen in front of the fire if you'd like?" It was as if he enjoyed keeping her off balance. She didn't really mind. The game felt amazing.

"Great idea."

He stood and offered his hand. She rose and stepped to him. "You're so beautiful," he murmured and brushed a gentle kiss across her forehead, then moved to the soft ivory flesh of her neck. The calm she'd gathered shattered. He reclaimed her lips, demanding more this time. She was shocked at her eager response to his lips caressing hers.

Jacks whispered, "You're incredible. Your body feels amazing in my arms." His mouth found hers again. Her knees weakened, and she was overwhelmed by her sensual response to his urgent and exploratory kiss. The contact sent a shock wave of pleasure through her body.

Jennifer felt his erection press against her. She fought to control the dizzying current racing through her. An invisible blanket of lava-like heat engulfed her. Waves of ecstasy surged through her. She wanted him to touch all of her. Her heartbeat hammered in her ears.

His touch lit a sexual fire. There was a dreamy intimacy to the kiss that turned raw and primal. She felt the tingling growing as he pushed her further in response. Never had a man made her climb this fast with a kiss. Soon she felt the release coming. She clung to him. Her head was spinning. The kiss ignited her soul. She was consumed by raw passion. His lips seared a path down her neck before he claimed her lips again, the kiss slow, thorough, and sexually charged.

He held her close. Continued to caress her with small kisses.

She was afraid to open her eyes. What on earth had she done? What would he think of her? She might as well have lain on the floor and said, "Take me, I'm desperate. How about a good time?"

"Sorry, I got carried away. You seem to have that effect on me. You okay?" Jacks asked.

"Shall we have lunch?"

She caught his grin and dashed past him toward the kitchen.

"Is there something I can do to help?"

Jennifer caught the shortness in her tone, but couldn't control it. "I think I have everything in hand."

He walked in front of her. "What's the matter?" When she didn't look up, he gently lifted her chin with his index finger until their eyes met. "Talk to me."

"I, well, never mind."

"Oh, no, you don't." When their eyes met again, he said, "Okay, I kissed you. You melted in my arms. Is that the problem? For the record, any damage you've done to my manhood has more than been repaired."

"It's not funny. I'm not the kind of woman who kisses every man she meets, much less has an—"

When she stuttered, he said, "Has a mind-blowing experience. It was mind-blowing, right?" His eyes sparkled. He bit his bottom lip. She could tell he was trying very hard not to laugh.

"That's not the point."

He stepped close again. "Okay, now we're getting someplace. So, it was mind-blowing?"

"Like I said, that's not the point. I'm not easy. I don't let just any man touch me."

He could see the tears welling up, "Oh, sweetheart. I didn't think that at all." He led her to the window bench. When they were seated, he continued, "It never crossed my mind that you were a pushover."

"You have so much experience. You must have had dozens of women. That's all."

"So now I'm easy.

"That isn't what I meant either, and you know it."

She was trying to compose herself, but he continued. "I've got you rattled, don't I?"

"No."

"People don't get you rattled, do they?"

"No."

He pulled her on his lap. "Beautiful, I couldn't stop myself when you reacted that way. It's never happened to me before. It was marvelous and incredibly sexy. I can kiss you one more time. We can see if it happens again."

"Kiss me again, please," she said in a weak and tremulous whisper.

His lips recaptured hers, demanding more this time. The kiss was urgent and exploratory. He fisted her hair. He forced her lips open with his thrusting tongue.

Jennifer's pulse skyrocketed as his lips descended. Her knees weakened. She surrendered fully to the passion of the kiss. The room spun.

Raising his mouth from hers, he gazed into her eyes, and placed his forehead against hers. "Again?"

Jennifer wasn't sure what to do. She wanted more than kisses, but it was too soon. She was having trouble catching her breath. Jacks' hard-on pulsed against her.

It was as if Jacks read her mind. He kissed her on the nose and smiled. "I don't know about you, but I think I need more cider."

****

Jacks enjoyed Jennifer's movements as they cleared away the dishes. He fought the desire to reach out, tussle her curls, and capture her lips again. Yep, she was sexy. Sexy and incredibly naïve. He'd miss her when he deployed. If they made love, there'd be a connection. She wasn't the type of woman to have casual sex. That had been the only thing that stopped him from pushing her further in the kiss earlier. *Stop now. Run. All women are trouble.* Mentally, Jacks shook his head. He'd worry about that later.

It didn't take long for thoughts of taking Jennifer

upstairs to return. They cuddled on the sofa and tried to watch a movie. Jacks stroked her arm with his fingertips and played with her long auburn curls. Their kisses began short and gentle but quickly turned long and hot.

The movie was forgotten when she slid onto his lap and ran her hands around his neck. Their bodies seemed to melt together. He released the clip in her hair and buried his face in the mass of curls. The scent of fresh-baked bread invited him. Jacks wanted to explore her body, claim her as his. At the same time, the thought scared the hell out of him. "I better go while there's a break in the storm."

"Which storm are you referring to, sailor?" Jennifer asked, biting her lip.

The sensual act had his already hard cock screaming for relief. "Believe the one outside has nothing on the one in here, my sweet." Her swollen lips and tousled hair called to him. But he wasn't ready to take the next step. The connection was already so strong. Once he made love with Jennifer there would be no going back.

Jennifer took a drink from her glass and licked her lips. "If you must," Jennifer purred and accented her comment with a wink that shot straight to his heart.

"You are an evil woman. I mean that in the best way possible." He placed a gentle kiss on her forehead. "I'll call you tomorrow."

****

Jacks' lips were still warm and moist from their kisses as he drove home. Even in remembrance, he felt the intimacy. This was going to be an exceptionally long night. He needed a diversion. And he knew exactly what to do; call his parents. He hit the button on his steering wheel. "Call Mom," Jacks said into the air.

As the number dialed, a truck pulling onto the highway behind him caught his eye. It seemed familiar, but here had he seen it? When his father answered the phone, the truck was forgotten.

"Hello," Admiral Williams said. "How are you, son?"

"I'm good, getting settled in my new place. You know the drill; heavy schedules prior to deployment. Is Mom with you?"

"Yes. I'll put you on speaker."

"Before you do, have you heard from Donna?" Jacks asked and turned his windshield wipers on high.

"Yes. She called wanting money to fix her car. Did she call you?"

"Yes, sir."

"I gather you sent her a check." He could hear the disappointment in his father's voice. Based on Jacks' past behavior, he had reason to doubt him. He'd folded and sent her money before.

"I didn't, told her the bank was closed, reminded her you and Mom put her through nursing school. As well as she received the divorce settlement she asked for and not to call me again."

"I'm proud of you, son. I know it's been a rough couple of years. I'll put the phone on speaker so you can talk with your mom."

"Good. I'm settled in my new place, working quite a bit. I've met someone." He was ready for the pause. He knew his past choices in women gave his parents ample reason to be skeptical.

There was no response, so he continued, "I think you'll like her. She's an Air Force Colonel, a psychologist, has her Ph.D. She was married for about twenty years. She divorced about the same time as me, and under the same circumstances. She's a friend of Brandon and his wife. That's how we met.

"How long have you been dating?"

"A month or so. She has twin daughters I haven't met. She hasn't dated since her divorce."

"Sounds like the woman has her priories straight."

"What's her name?" Henry asked.

"Dr. Jennifer Ryan."

"Be careful, son," his mom said. Jacks could visualize the look of concern even over the phone.

"Don't worry, she's not like Donna, and we're moving very slowly." Jacks left out Jennifer knew his mother was an author and wasn't sure why he left that out.

"Good."

He shifted the conversation to the reason for his call. "Is the cottage at Slaughter's Beach available for the Thanksgiving holiday?"

"Your mom and I were hoping to start a new tradition by celebrating the holiday there this year. Will that work?" Henry asked.

"Sure. Do you mind if I bring Jennifer? Her daughters will be with their dad."

"Of course, bring her along," Martha said.

"Great, talk with you soon."

Jacks wasn't sure why he wanted his family to meet Jennifer. Why was it important for them to like her? Was he headed down a slippery slope to a serious relationship? He laughed and shoved the thoughts away. A meaningful relationship; how stupid of him to even consider it at this point. He'd enjoy Jennifer until he deployed. That's all it was, right? Why did the thought of leaving her make him sad?

Chapter Eight

"I have to work tonight; would you like to do something tomorrow?" Jacks asked as they walked toward the restaurant parking lot.

"Sure. Do you have a suggestion?" Jennifer asked.

He stopped under an oak tree and took her hand. "I was thinking maybe the aquarium in Virginia Beach?"

Jennifer licked her lips. The simple action made his cock hard.

"Wonderful. I'll pack a picnic. There're great spots to spread out a blanket and enjoy a leisurely lunch."

Visions of making love to Jennifer in the woods flooded his mind. "A picnic sounds great. I'll pick you up at nine."

"That works."

As they walked toward the cars, Jacks asked, "What's on your agenda for the rest of the day?"

"Kimberly and I are going shopping at the Harley dealership. I'm going to get clothing for the bike ride next week."

Jacks' libido shot up like a rocket again. "Knee-high leather boots on your list?"

She slid her sunglasses down her nose. Looked over them at Jacks and winked. "Is there a special color you have in mind?"

"No. Anything works." The woman had no idea the effect she had on him. The smile knocked him out. He needed her. Sleeping alone was driving him mad.

"You want me in leather?" she asked with a grin. "Is there something I should know about you from a psychological standpoint?" She smiled and slid her sunglasses in place.

"No. I'm thinking totally of your comfort. Leather pants and chaps are both nice and warm for rides." *Nice will be taking the leathers off you, ever so slowly.* He stepped toward her, placed a quick kiss on her lips. "Beautiful, I've got to work. See you in the morning."

Jennifer laughed. "That's all the kiss I get?" She stuck out her bottom lip and flashed a come-and-take-me smile.

"We'll continue this conversation tomorrow."

"As you wish," she purred.

All the way back to work, flashes of Jennifer in leather boots, her body molded to his on the motorcycle kept him hot as hell. Damn, the woman was going to drive him crazy until he took her to bed. He would take her to bed. It was a matter of time. *Isn't it?* a small voice in his mind whispered.

****

Jennifer was telling Kimberly about her conversation with Jacks as they walked into the dealership. "Tried to play it off like he was thinking only about my welfare. He said leather pants and chaps are warmer on a ride."

Kimberly chuckled. "I understand. No matter what Brandon's doing, all I must do is bring up my leather boots. I've immediately got his undivided attention."

"Men and leather. It's an age-old fantasy."

They moved to the counter where a gray-haired man with a beard and ponytail looked up. "Hey Kimberly."

"Hi. This is Jennifer. She needs gear for a fund raiser ride up the coast next month."

"I'm sure Marla can fix you up. Speak of the devil; here she comes now."

"What did I do now?" a tall blonde woman said approaching the front of the store. "Good to see you, Kimberly."

"You, too. This is my friend Jennifer. She needs clothes for a ride up the coast."

"Well, I can fix you up. Do you have a color in mind?"

"No, not really," Jennifer answered.

"Let's try black. Most guys love a woman in black," Marla said with a laugh.

"There's something about women in leather all men love," Jennifer added.

"Let's start with pants. I have these and love them." Marla turned a full circle and showed off her pants. "Are you an eight?"

"On a good day. You better bring a ten."

The three ladies chatted as they worked their way around the women's section.

"I think we have at least one of everything you need. The dressing room is this way," Marla said and headed toward the back of the store.

"Try these," Kimberly said, handing her friend a pair of pants, T-shirt, and a vest.

In the dressing room, Jennifer slipped into the soft leather. "These feel great."

"Come out and show us," Kimberly said.

"Okay." Jennifer poked her head between the curtains and looked around before exiting the dressing room. She turned and studied herself as Marla tightened the back laces of the pants.

"These certainly are low on my hips." Jennifer couldn't figure out why she was whispering.

"You've got the body, show it off, girlfriend," Kimberly said as she helped lace the vest. "This looks killer. You're going to have Jacks spellbound."

Jennifer looked over her shoulder in the mirror. She was stunned at the reflection. "Wow. What else do I need?"

Soon she was in front of the mirror again decked out in pants, studded leather chaps, vest, jacket, and black knee boots. "I can't believe it's me."

Kimberly laughed. "Jacks is going to be speechless. What are you grinning about?"

"What Phillip would say? Maybe this is the variety he was talking about."

Kimberly smiled at her friend. "You're evil."

"Yes. But it's so much fun," Jennifer replied, checking her reflection in the mirror one more time.

****

"Ready for your first ride?" Jacks asked, checking out Jennifer's outfit. The jeans clung to her hips, and the black leather lace-up vest highlighted her ample breasts. The sight made his heart beat faster.

"Sure. It's a beautiful bike. I love the American flag. Jennifer slowly ran her fingertips the full length of the bike.

It was one of the most sensual things Jacks had ever seen. "Thanks. A few reminders before we head out. Your seat is heated. If you get cold, turn this knob. Like we discussed, the communication is set up in the helmet. Any questions?"

"Nope, I think I remember everything," Jennifer

used her nails to walk up Jacks chest. "You're a great teacher."

Jacks drew her tight into his arms. Her breath quickened against his neck and his sexual intoxication surged. He leaned in to kiss her but at the last second placed his lips on her forehead and whispered, "You keep those beautiful long legs of yours gripping mine."

"I can do that, Sailor," Jennifer whispered and accented her action with a wink.

Her sexy grin made his toes tingle and his cock hard. "Damn, woman, you're going to be the death of me."

"Wh-a-t?" The question came out in three long syllables.

"Don't play innocent with me. You know exactly what you're doing."

"You want me to stop?" The statement was delivered with her killer smile.

Jacks' response was to flip the foot peddle down and mount the bike. Jennifer climbed on behind him. Both secured their helmets.

"You ready?"

"Yep. Where we headed?"

"Over the Chesapeake Bay Bridge to the Great Mashipongo Clam Shack. They have the best seafood for miles."

"Great. Seafood is always good. Plus, I love driving across the bridge. The girls and I often drive to the halfway point and have lunch. We love to watch for dolphins playing in the water. We tried fishing a couple of times but weren't successful." Jennifer shifted forward and closer to Jacks' butt.

Jacks' cock was already hard, and her movement sent his sexual fantasies flying. He had to find something to say. "Have you ever been deep sea fishing?"

"Not one of my finer moments. I spent most of the trip with my head between my legs to stop from being sick. The kids caught fish. I managed to pull it together by the time we got home so I could cook."

Jacks slowed the bike and passed through the toll booth. He gunned the engine and took off across the bridge.

"Wow," Jennifer whispered.

"You okay back there?"

"This is amazing. It's a combination of exhilaration, fear, and pleasure all at once."

Jacks reached back with his right hand and stroked Jennifer's thigh. "It can be an experience that can change you forever."

"Now I understand the bumper sticker I saw. You never see a motorcycle parked in front of a psychiatrist's office. This is great therapy."

Jacks hit the throttle, and the speed gauge moved to *90* before he began to slow the bike. Jennifer's response was to hold tighter. That was fine with him. Somehow a ride would never be the same without Jennifer behind him.

****

Jennifer's cell phone rang, and she hit the answer button on her steering wheel. "Hello, this is Dr. Ryan."

"Good morning, beautiful."

Her stomach turned at the sound of the voice. "Phillip. How are Lisa and the baby?"

"We're all good."

She was irked by his cool, aloof manner. "What do you want?" *How could the jerk miss the unfriendliness in her tone?*

91

"Can you trade weekends with me?"

"You mean this coming weekend?" Jennifer replied and took a drink from her mug of tea.

"Yes."

"Sorry, I can't."

"Are you going out of town?"

"I have plans. I was going to call Lisa about the girl's activities. No need to exchange much since they have clothes at your house."

"I can swing by your place and pick them up."

"No need. We can do the exchange at school."

"Okay." The disappointment came through loud and clear in his voice.

"I'll send Lisa an email with the girls' schedule. There's the usual dance class on Friday and soccer practice before a birthday party on Saturday. I have the invitations and gifts."

"What are you doing this weekend?" Phillip asked again.

"My personal life is my business. Given we're divorced, you don't need to know anything about my plans." Anger crept up her spine.

"It does if it impacts *my* daughters!"

Jennifer took a deep breath. *Don't let him ruin your good mood.* "Phillip, when something I do might impact our children, I'll be sure to let you know."

"I pay three grand a month in child support that gives me rights," his anger seemed to jump from the speaker.

Her body stiffened at the remark. Her tight mental control burst. She had a death grip on the steering wheel. "Oh no! You don't get to go there. You pushed for the divorce and agreed to the terms. Don't even try to throw that crap in my face. When I invite someone into my life, you'll know when I want you to. You're the one who went down that road first. I like Lisa. She and I are building a relationship for the benefit of the twins. Tell Lisa hello," was her parting comment as she disconnected the call.

****

Jennifer grabbed her purse and called upstairs. "Madison, Morgan, you ready?"

"Yes, Mom, we're on the way," Morgan said as both girls ran downstairs.

"Put your things for the weekend in the bag on the table. Your gifts for Tanya are there, too."

"Okay," the girls chimed in.

"Let's go; your dad and Lisa will be waiting," Jennifer said, setting the alarm. The girls and their mother sang along with the radio as they headed to school.

In the parking lot, Phillip leaned against his car.

"Mom, what's wrong with Dad? He looks angry," Madison said as they got out of the car.

"Who knows?" She tried to squash the sarcasm in her tone. "Go say hello. I love you. Have fun this weekend; you can call me anytime." *Don't react to Phillip—that's what he wants.* She repeated as a mental mantra.

"Okay, I love you too," Morgan said and hugged her goodbye.

"See you Tuesday afternoon. Love you, Mommy," Madison said when it was her turn.

The three walked to where Phillip stood. "Hello, Daddy," both girls said as they sat their bags on the ground.

Phillip hugged them. "How are my girls today?"

"Good," Morgan said.

"Ready for school to be out," Madison added.

"I'll be here at three thirty to pick you up, head into school. I'll put your things in the trunk."

"Bye," Morgan and Madison said in unison. They looked both ways and followed the crosswalk to the school entrance.

Jennifer waved to the girls before turning to Phillip. "Here are the girls' gifts for the birthday party." She handed him two brightly decorated gift bags with dancing cartoon dachshunds. "Where is Lisa?" Jennifer asked.

"She stayed home; I needed to talk to you. You certainly look good. Is that a new sweater?"

"What do you want?" Jennifer couldn't fathom how he missed the anger growing in her voice.

"I want to know about your plans for the weekend. Are you going away with that damn Navy Commander? The one you've been meeting for lunch at the O Club?" His curt voice lashed out at her.

"I'm not going through this again. The girls are with you this weekend. Enjoy your family," Jennifer said, turned, and began walking toward her car.

Phillip grabbed her arm and spun her around. "We aren't done! I have every right to know if *some* pervert is around my children. What if the two of you are having sex and *my* daughters walk in?"

Jennifer jerked her arm away and laughed. "You told me once you wanted me to show emotion, act like other women would." She stepped inches from Phillip and threw her words like stones. "Listen closely, you lousy son-of-a-bitch, this is the last time we'll have this conversation. Do you understand me? Don't ever touch me."

She pushed him square in his chest with her hand. Her eyes clawed at him like talons. "Unlike you, not all men have trouble keeping it in their pants. It's my decision if I choose to take someone into my bed. In case you forgot, I was the faithful one in our marriage. There isn't a revolving door on my bedroom. I don't have to have a man in my life to be happy. It's my choice." Jennifer slipped her hands into her pockets to stop from slapping Phillip. "Besides, you don't want me as an enemy."

"What are you talking about?" Confusion filled his eyes, and his mouth opened and closed like a fish.

The look on his face told her everything. "You have a girlfriend. I can read you like a book, same chapter and verse. I recognize the signs I missed when we were married.

"Really, I saw you step out and take a call during the girls' party. I could tell by your tone of voice it wasn't business. Plus, Madison mentioned your coming home late. All it takes is for me to place a bit of doubt in Lisa's mind, and you would be out on your ass. Don't push me, you'll lose again."

She turned and walked to her car, leaving a shell-shocked Phillip leaning on his trunk. She started her car, backed out of the parking place, put the car in drive, and gently pulled toward the exit of the parking lot. Phillip waved for her to stop. Against her better judgement, she did.

His words began as soon as the window cracked an inch. "I'm sorry, just the thought of you with another man makes me crazy."

"Well, welcome to what used to be my world. This is what it was like for me all those times you were with your little sluts, and let me tell you, the pain never gets any easier. You're the one who made a mockery of our marriage. That's the reason I finally agreed to the divorce. Pastor Bell and I discussed how your adultery invalidated our vows. You made your bed; now lie in it. Leave me the fuck out of this. Don't flatter yourself to think you'll ever be back in mine."

"Wait, you told Pastor Bell about that? How can I ever go back to church with him knowing?"

She laughed and shook her head. "You complained about going. I gathered you wouldn't care. Besides, if you don't want people to know what you're doing; it's the wrong thing to do. Isn't that what you told the Sunday school class during one of your lessons? Not to mention you haven't been in months."

"Tell me you don't love me."

Jennifer smiled on the inside. *Phillip was shifting tactics. He was, if nothing else, predictable.* "Unfortunately, a part of me will always love you because of our daughters. But you killed any true love I felt. I thought I was a failure the first time you slept around. You gave me your word it would never happen again. But that was another lie. Did you think I didn't know?"

She continued when Phillip stared at her speechless, mouth open.

"Do you think I insisted on condoms because I really didn't want to take birth control?" She smiled and laughed. "I was on the pill. I didn't want a sexually transmitted disease because you didn't use a condom with your special friends. And please don't insult my intelligence by saying you *always* used protection. Lisa's pregnancy certainly disproves that, or perhaps you planned it."

When he tried to speak, Jennifer held up her hand.

"If I decide to spend the weekend fucking my brains out, that's my choice. Phillip, go to counseling and make a life with Lisa. She loves you. You've got it made with her. Send the girls' things with them to school on Tuesday."

Jennifer rolled up her window and drove away. She turned on the radio and tried to relax. She was furious. Jacks would be at her house in an hour. She had to change her mood. Phillip had ruined enough of her life. She'd leave him and the crappy mood in the rear-view mirror.

Chapter Nine

Jennifer was over her ex-husband's shenanigans when she opened the door for Jacks. "Hello, handsome."

"Good morning. Red certainly is your color." He kissed her left cheek. "You look wonderful in that sweater."

She stepped to his left and said, "Come in. I made coffee and cinnamon buns."

"That can wait." Jacks placed his hands on her shoulders, looked into her eyes, leaned in, and brushed his lips over hers.

She stepped into his arms and ran her hands up his chest and around his neck. He leaned in and kissed her. As the passion built, she responded to his sexual hunger. He stroked her hair and back. She caressed his neck with her fingertips. When his lips parted, Jennifer deepened the kiss. It took every bit of her control to break the embrace.

"I think we better have coffee. If we don't, I may not be responsible for my actions," Jacks said as he swept the hair from her face.

"I agree."

****

Jennifer's body ached for his touch. Jacks seemed to be holding back, and she wasn't sure why. Maybe he didn't intend to take her to bed before he deployed. She'd seen the smoldering flame in his eyes. Felt his

98

excitement pressed against her. Perhaps all he wanted was someone to hang out with. But it didn't feel that way.

Whatever it was, she was going to take charge. She wanted Jackson Williams, and she would have him, even if it meant issuing a challenge in the form of a dare.

Jennifer was nervous and excited at the same time. She'd gone on several motorcycle rides with Jacks, slowly building her confidence. She knew how to mold her body to his and lean into the curves when necessary. But here she was on US129, one day away from riding the infamous Tail of the Dragon. Three hundred eighteen turns in eleven miles.

The Great Smoky Mountains supplied breathtaking scenery. The leaves were changing into their multicolor fall tones. As Mother Nature freed the leaves from their summer home, they floated to the ground, continuing the circle of life. They'd seen wildlife along the way as well.

****

Jacks took Jennifer's hand. "Come on, I want you to meet my brothers."

"Okay," she said.

Jacks smiled and kissed Jennifer on the nose. "You scared?"

"Sorta, I guess. What if they don't like me?" Jennifer said as she squeezed his hand.

"Well, that isn't going to happen. Think of them as the two mischievous little boys from Mom's books," Jacks suggested as they walked down the gravel path.

Jennifer chuckled. "Not sure that'll work. I don't want to view you that way. It's creepy given my level of interest." She kissed his cheek.

"Really? Save that thought for later. Come on, they

won't bite. Well, maybe Alex, he's short on manners sometimes. But he's had all his shots." He took her hand and led her toward a group of bikers.

Two men stepped from the group.

It didn't matter. Jennifer could have picked them out of a crowd. Each had their own look, but the mannerisms were there. The confident stride, wide smile, and eyes that could make a woman melt. Despite their differences, all three were handsome, successful men.

Max's full beard and waist-length light-brown hair suited him. His jeans were tattered and worn. He sported a *Legalize Marijuana* T-shirt. No one would guess he was the son of Admiral Williams or a New York Times best-selling author. She wondered if his military intrigue and spy novels kept his father up at night.

Alex was the opposite. His jeans still held the pressed crease; his blond hair was cut in the military high and tight. Under his black leather jacket was a button-up powder blue dress shirt. He looked like he'd stepped off the cover of a men's fashion magazine.

Jennifer smiled when the brothers embraced and exchanged hellos.

Alex released his brother and turned his attention to Jennifer. "You must be Jennifer."

She smiled as he closed her in his arms.

"Hey, get your hands off my girl," Jacks said.

"I'm only saying hello." Alex stepped back but didn't let go.

"My turn," Max chimed in. He playfully shoved Alex out of the way. "You have to excuse my brothers. They have no manners," Max continued as he took Jennifer's hand and kissed it. "It's a pleasure to meet you."

"Hello," Jennifer managed to say as Max led her away. Alex was holding Jacks at bay.

"I have one question," he said but didn't wait for a response. "What do you see in my much older brother?"

"I-I…" Jennifer tried to answer but felt like she'd been hit by a truck load of boyish charm. The two of them were having fun at Jacks' expense. But he seemed to be enjoying it.

"All right, back the hell off, both of you. Get your own woman," Jacks said, taking Jennifer's hand from Max. He slipped his arm around her waist, pulled her to him. "Sweetie, sorry, my baby brothers are pigs."

"It's okay," she said, laughing.

"Wait," Max said, holding up his hands. "Let's be gentlemen about this. Now that she's met us all. Maybe she'd like to change her mind."

To join the banter, Jennifer paused for a second before responding and looked at each of them. "Sorry, guys. I'm incredibly happy with my choice." She kissed Jacks on the cheek and ran her hand down his chest.

Max kicked the dirt like a little boy who'd lost his favorite truck. Jennifer watched as his grin grew. "Okay. Do you have a sister?"

"Sorry," Jennifer said, shrugging her shoulders.

Jacks said, "They'll both be in love by sundown."

"And happily, single in the morning. All I might lose is a few hours' sleep," Max added as the group headed toward the outdoor bar.

"See, like me, they like you," Jacks whispered as they walked.

Jennifer turned to face him, kissed his neck, and whispered, "Is that what it is—you just *like* me?" She raised an eyebrow in question.

Her actions and the sultry tone left him breathless. Jacks took her jaw in both his palms. His words brushed over her lips. "Oh, yes, sexy. I like you a lot." Panic enveloped Jacks. *Hell, yes, he liked her. Dammit, he loved her.* But all he could say was, "You want a drink?"

"Sure."

He read the disappointment loud and clear in her tone.

****

Jennifer wasn't sure what to do. She noticed Kimberly waving from a table. "Jacks, Kimberly has a table by the tree. I'll meet you guys over there." She pointed to their left.

"What would you like to drink?"

"Surprise me," Jennifer said and brushed her lips over Jacks'. The warmth made her smile, but instantly doubt began to sink in.

"They're quite a group, aren't they?" Kimberly asked, sipping her drink.

Jennifer watched the three men laughing at the bar, ordering drinks. "Really. They seem happy to see each other."

"Yep. The family's awfully close. Did you know they grew up with Brandon's kids?"

"No."

"Brandon and Henry have been friends since the Persian Gulf War."

Jacks turned and smiled at Jennifer. It took her breath away. The man was amazing. She smiled and blew him a kiss. He put his hand to his chest, backed up and shot her a sexy wink.

"Hey. You, okay?" Kimberly asked.

"What?" Jennifer answered on autopilot.

Kimberly smiled and raised an eyebrow. "You're in love with him, aren't you?"

"He—he…" Jennifer shook her head and smiled. "I don't know. He makes me happy." She was deciding what to say when thankfully, the men arrived with drinks.

"Hello, beautiful," Jacks whispered. As he slipped the cup into her hand, his fingers brushed hers.

"Thanks." Jennifer sipped her drink. Was she in love with Jacks? She knew she was; that was the problem. The redeeming quality was he'd deploy soon, and she'd have time to think the situation through, but for tonight she'd have fun. Could she follow through with her plan? Her knees were weak at the thought. What if Jacks thought she was frigid too? Could Phillip be right?

Chapter Ten

Jacks knocked on Jennifer's hotel room door. When she opened it, he leaned in and brushed his lips over hers. "I'm heading to have a drink with my brothers. Wanna join me?"

"I'm going to take a shower. Stop by when you're done. I have a bottle of wine chilling." She pointed toward a nightstand. "Kimberly had a box of my things in her car. I've got cheese and crackers, too. If you're hungry, that is."

Jacks stepped toward her and teased her lips with his tongue. "You know I could meet my brothers later."

Jennifer put her hand on his chest. "No. See your brothers. I'll be right here waiting."

"If you insist." Jacks placed a kiss on her forehead. Man, he wanted her. There was an internal war raging. The slow seduction was fun, but it was making him crazy, especially with four hours of her body molded to his on the bike.

He strolled into the bar. His brothers were at a table in the back. Alex was chatting up the waitress. Max was typing on his laptop. Some things never changed.

As he approached the table, the waitress walked away. "Losing your charm? Or did you already get her phone number?"

Alex stood and hugged his brother. "Good to see you. Where's your lovely passenger" He asked, looking over his brother's shoulder.

"She's taking a shower."

"Getting ready for you? How much is the entry fee for that sexy thing?" Max asked with a laugh.

Jacks shot out of the chair, grabbed Max by his jacket, and yanked him out of his chair. His anger surprised even him. "It's not like that. She's different," he said, his tone sharp and hostile.

Alex put a hand on each one of their chests and pushed them apart. "Play nice, boys. I'm not driving anyone to the hospital tonight. You'll bleed until tomorrow." Jacks didn't miss the great impression of their mother.

"Sorry, man. I didn't know it was serious," Max said as he straightened his shirt.

"I didn't say it was serious. Jennifer's not a weekend plaything. She's special. That's all."

"Oh," Alex said in an exaggerated fashion.

Jacks caught the visual exchange between his brothers and asked, "What does that mean?"

Max held up his hands. "Nothing, man, it's all cool."

"Marie, honey, would you bring my brother a scotch on the rocks?" Alex asked the waitress as she passed by the table. "And another round for us," he added, pointing to the empty glasses on the table.

"Sure."

"Seriously, Jennifer seems nice," Max said.

"At the risk of being slugged, I'd like to say, brother, she's extremely easy to look at. Shame she doesn't have a sister."

Jacks sipped his drink. Jennifer was sexy and hot in her leather chaps and boots. Damn, she was hot in anything.

The friendly banter continued as the brothers polished off another couple of drinks.

Jacks stood and threw money on the table. "As pleasant as sitting around chatting with you two losers might be, I gotta go. Jennifer asked me to stop by."

Alex nearly choked on his drink. "You two are in separate rooms? What the fuck, big brother? Haven't closed the deal? You were so my hero."

"Need some help?" Max said as he stood.

"Go screw yourselves." Jacks shoved his hands in his jacket pockets and headed out of the bar. What was going on with Jennifer? He'd never dated anyone this long and not scored. He was drunk enough to still be pissed by his brothers' teasing as he knocked on Jennifer's door. He needed to be with her. Touch her body as only her lover could.

"Hey, sailor," she said from behind the slightly opened door.

"Hi," he said.

"You want to come in?"

"Sure."

Jennifer crooked her finger. "Well?"

Jacks sauntered into the room. Jennifer closed and locked the door. He took the visual trip from the long curls flowing over her breasts to the five-inch purple heels and back again. The robe brushed her ankles and gave a glimpse of a short purple sheer gown and black lace-trimmed stockings. He licked his lips.

She took three steps to him and ran her nails through his hair. Her lips brushed against his as she spoke. "I hope you don't mind aggressive women." She pushed him against the door with her body. Leaned in and used the velvet warmth of her tongue to caress his lips. The kiss was a smoldering heat that joined metals. It was as much of a challenge as a reward.

Jennifer kissed his cheek and used her tongue to draw a line to the hollow of his neck. She stroked his arms with her nails. A shudder passed through him.

Jacks fought to regain his composure. His whiskey buzz blending with her mouth-watering merlot was intoxicating.

She pressed against him. "You didn't answer my question. Or do I need to dare you to kiss me again?"

"What, huh?"

"Do you like aggressive women?" Her voice was low and sultry.

"Oh, yeah, sexy." He took her face in his hands. "You're full of surprises. Let me look at you."

Jennifer stepped away. Turned in a full circle and slid the silk robe off her shoulders. It puddled around her high heels. He stepped to her and ran his hands under the sheer fabric and caressed the warm flesh. With a fingertip, he traced a line from her waist to the lace top of her stockings. His stomach fluttered; he was a little boy at Christmas, not sure what to unwrap first.

She walked her fingers up his chest, unbuttoned his shirt, ran her hands inside the fabric, and whispered, "Jacks, I want you naked. I *need* to feel your skin on mine."

Her voice was smooth and smoky like a fine cigar. Her eyes were pools of deep, dark purple, and her chest rose and fell in anticipation.

She ran her tongue around his nipple and gently nibbled. His erection throbbed as she kissed her way down his abdomen with exaggerated, slow precision. She reached for his belt, and he heard his voice tremble,

"I can help you with that."

She shook her head; curls brushed his stomach, adding yet another layer of arousal.

His body vibrated when Jennifer unbuttoned his fly, reached inside, and freed his throbbing erection. His knees went weak when she shot him a brief glance and licked her lips. She closed her mouth around him as he mumbled something even incoherent to him. His hands automatically fisted her curls.

"Jennifer, baby, that feels amazing," he said between gasps. Jacks shifted his weight against the door to prevent falling. She kissed her way up his chest.

When their eyes met, she was smiling. "You want to sit down?"

He pulled her to him and crushed her mouth with his. His passion drove him like a madman. He kissed her deep and hard. Running his hand along her skin, he found her center and stroked as he moved his mouth to her breasts. He feasted like a starving man. "Take the gown off, or I'll rip it off," Jacks didn't recognize the voice that demanded her to act.

"As you wish." She pulled the gown over her head and tossed it away.

She stood before him in a thong, stockings, and heels. "Where do I start?" he whispered.

"Anywhere you like. I'm all yours. How would you like me?"

He looked to the ceiling and mouthed, "Thank you." He kicked off his shoes and removed his pants. Jacks took her hand and kissed her palm. "I want all of you, every lovely inch. He cupped her butt with his hands pulling her against him. "You certainly surprised me, sexy."

"Good. That's exactly what I planned. But I'm just getting started."

"Do I dare ask what else you have in mind?"

"You could take off my heels and stockings." Jennifer turned, grabbed a chair, and straddled it backward.

"Saints be praised." He dropped to one knee and tried to unbuckle the strap. His hands were unsteady.

"You can slip them off," she whispered.

With the shoes off, he rolled the silk and lace down first one leg and then the other. "Take off the panties. Let me watch."

She stood, slipped her thumbs in the small strips of elastic, and inched them toward the floor.

Sweet torture. He didn't want the show to stop. At the same time, it was the only scrap of material between them. When she stood naked before him, emotions flooded his mind. "Come here, beautiful." He closed her in his arms and held tight. "You're amazing. I hate to be a killjoy, but I don't have condoms."

"I do, in the nightstand," she whispered, kissing him on the neck.

He lifted and placed her on the bed and lay beside her. "Now, where were we?"

"About right here." She shifted, forced him on his back, and popped a cube of ice in her mouth from a glass on the nightstand. She had his full attention as she licked her way to his erection and closed her mouth around it. Jacks' eyes shot open when her warmth turned ice cold. Her eyes met his and she let the small piece of ice roll to the end of her tongue. "You are an evil, evil woman."

"You want me to stop?'

"Don't get carried away. I meant it as a

compliment."

Her response was to take him again and continue the shift from hot to cold. Jacks felt the end coming. He knew she'd stop. There'd never been a woman who'd taken him to the end. Damn, it felt wonderful. She'd stop any minute. He'd enjoy it a bit more and the—his thoughts stopped as she took him over the edge. As his mind cleared, his hands were buried in her hair as his body reveled in the aftershocks. He felt her slide up his body.

"Hi," was all Jennifer said. She was grinning like the cat that swallowed the proverbial canary.

"Hi, yourself," he managed to mumble.

"I'll be right back," Jennifer said as she climbed from the bed. She returned dressed in her robe, carrying two glasses of wine. She sat cross-legged on the bed and offered one. "Here you go."

"Thanks. Maybe in a minute. I need to catch my breath."

She sipped her wine. The grin was magnificent, and her eyes sparkled.

"Damn proud of yourself, aren't you?"

"Sure, what woman wouldn't enjoy seeing her lover totally sated? You are, satisfied, aren't you?" she added with a giggle.

"Oh, baby, you have no idea. Come here," he said as he opened his arms.

She set the glasses on the nightstand, crawled into his arms, and put her head on his shoulder.

Jacks kissed her on the top of her head. "I must tell you, I'm surprised. I knew you were responsive. But I didn't see you as a sex vixen."

"It's probably bad to say this, but you can thank my

ex. He took a great deal of time teaching me that trick and others."

Jacks laughed so hard his chest hurt. "Maybe I should send him a thank you note."

Jennifer laughed, too. She shifted to sitting and grabbed a glass of wine.

"I'd love to see his face when he opened it. I've always had a healthy attitude about sex. My aunt told me most men wanted a wonderful cook and hostess in every room of the house except the bedroom. There they wanted a sweet and innocent sexual performer."

He kissed her knuckles and said, "I think you qualify on all points."

"Why thank you," Jennifer said, sipping her wine.

Jacks propped his head on his elbow and asked, "What other advice did your aunt give you?"

Jennifer leaned against the footboard. "Not to wait until a boy had me all tingly to decide to give away my virginity. Make the decision with a level head. Make it happen on my terms. Not in a back seat, but where I wanted. Make it special. So I decided to wait until Phillip and I were married."

Jacks almost spit his wine all over the bed. "What?"

"Phillip and I didn't have sex until our wedding night. He'd have been pissed, except it was his opportunity to take my *tabula rasa* and write on it what he wanted. He was a good teacher. He said I was a wonderful student."

"You've never had sex with anyone but Phillip?"

"Nope, you and I are halfway there. Is that a problem?"

"No. Not at all."

"I told you I'd never been kissed by anyone but

Phillip. Didn't you believe me?"

Jacks read her panic. He placed his wine on the nightstand and crawled to her. "Baby, I forgot. My mind was sailing that night. I was so lost in you. You had me so turned on. I'm surprised, that's all, and honored you picked me as your lover." He slipped the glass from her hand, and set it aside. Took her hands, "Jennifer, you are very special. Come be with me. Let me please you."

"As you wish," she purred.

****

Jennifer stretched out on the bed as she smiled at her lover.

Jacks stared down into her eyes and released the belt of her robe. With fingertips, he slipped both sides off her shoulders. Her heart began to pound when he lowered his mouth to her breast. "You're exquisite. I want to taste all of you."

She drew in a sharp breath when he licked and kissed his way down her body. She squirmed when he ran his fingertips down her body into her center.

"Yes, yes," she whispered.

"How about this, my sweet?" Jacks asked as he increased the speed and depth of his strokes. She grasped the sheet and moved against him.

"Yes, yes, don't stop, please. It feels so good."

"But I have so much more planned for you," he said and kissed his way down to her inner thigh. He traced a line with his tongue under her knee and continued up until he brushed his tongue against her throbbing peak. He increased his speed until he tasted her sweet relief.

"Jacks, please," she begged in a husky tone.

"Yes, what would you like?"

"Take me now. I need to feel you inside me." She

heard the whimper in her voice.

"I'll get there. I want you higher." Her body tingled as he used his tongue and hands to find pleasure points she never knew existed.

He kissed her body inch by inch until he faced her again. "I seem to recall you like me to kiss your neck…like this. Where is that sweet spot?" he breathed.

"Jacks," she screamed as she fell into a well of complete delight. "Please. I can't stand it anymore."

"Oh, baby, I'm just getting started. Will you look at me? I want to see those beautiful eyes when we become one."

Jennifer was pushed further into the pool of pleasure as stroke by stroke, he inched his way into her velvet glove. When he was buried in her, she felt the heat flow over him. The orgasms racked her body. She fought to breathe. Wave after wave of pleasure rushed through her body. She clawed at him.

She gazed into his eyes. He seemed to dare her to keep going. His hot breath flowed over her neck; she'd never been this high. His mouth found her nipple, and as he caressed it, she climaxed again. The rush of pleasure caught her off guard and her mind reeled.

Jacks slowed his strokes and whispered, "Yes, baby, yes." He joined her in the journey of total release.

****

"Wow," Jacks said when they were stretched out on the bed, fighting to catch their breath. He pulled her hand to his lips and kissed it.

"Really." Jennifer turned onto her side and smiled.

It made Jacks warm all over. The woman was amazing. "Great idea, wine and cheese."

Before she could respond, Jacks' phone rang. He

climbed from the bed and searched his pants. "Hello," he fought to control his breathing.

"Jacks, you okay," Kimberly asked.

"Sure. What's up?"

"Are you guys coming to dinner?"

He looked at his watch. "Kimberly," he mouthed to the sexy creature on the bed.

"Sure," he responded, but his thoughts were on his lover. She was sitting cross-legged in the middle of the bed, naked, drinking wine and licking her lips. He missed what Kimberly asked. "Sorry, what?"

"We're at the restaurant. Are you guys going to join us? We're getting ready to order."

"Yep, we'll be there in fifteen. Order for us, will you? Two big steaks, medium rare, baked potatoes, Caesar dressing on the salads, and water to drink. That should do it." He didn't wait for her to answer before he disconnected the call. "Come on, beautiful. Let's have dinner. I need my strength. My plans for the evening have changed drastically."

She climbed from the bed. "What, no night bike ride?" Jennifer asked as she traced a line with her nails from his neck to his belly button.

He grabbed her hand before she could go any lower. "Stop that."

"What?" She asked in four long syllables.

"Damn, woman, you are so bad." He pulled her to him and covered her mouth with his.

His hands explored her body. "You've got me hard again."

She stepped back, turned a circle, and asked, "So I guess the question is which hunger you want to quench first?"

"No question. I can eat cold steak." He lifted her on the bed, rolled on a condom, and took her hard and fast.

****

As they rode back toward Williamsburg, both were relaxed and sexually spent. Jennifer tightened her hold on Jacks' waist. When he reached back and patted her knee, her desire returned.

Jacks steered the motorcycle onto Highway 464. "What are your plans for Thanksgiving?"

"Don't really have any. Morgan and Madison will be with their father."

"Would you like to spend it with me?"

"Certainly. I'm even willing to cook. Would you like to stay at my house?" An excitement began to grow in her stomach.

"Perhaps, but I might have another plan. Would you like to go to the beach in Delaware?"

"That sounds like fun. I'm still happy to cook."

"My parents—" was all Jacks said before a truck swerved into their lane. It seemed to be trying to push them across all four lanes of traffic.

Jennifer's body automatically flowed with Jacks. He almost laid the bike down. Jennifer forced herself to relax and go with the movements. Jacks would not let anything happen to her. Her heart was pounding, and every muscle in her body tightened as she hung to Jacks' mid-section.

Jacks' breathing came in gulps as he slowed the bike and maneuvered it to the shoulder of the road. Jennifer found a strange humor in the string of four-syllable words she heard through the two-way communicator.

"Baby, you okay?" Jacks asked when the bike came to a stop.

"I think so," she said in jagged breaths as she climbed from the bike and removed her helmet.

Jacks did the same. He put his hands on his knees and slowed his breathing before he asked, "Did you see that jackass?"

"It's like he was trying to kill us. Do you think it was on purpose?" Jennifer answered quickly over her choking, beating heart.

"Did the truck look familiar to you?" Jacks asked, looking down the roadway.

"Don't think so. You?" She had to sit down. She collapsed on the grass.

Jacks sat down beside her. "It's like someplace in my subconscious; I've seen it before." Half teasing, he asked, "Phillip doesn't have a truck, does he?"

"Not that I know of." But the seed had been planted. Could Phillip hate her that much? "I'm sure he wouldn't do anything to hurt me," Jennifer said matter-of-factly, but who was she trying to convince, herself or Jacks?

He took her shaking hands in his. "I'm sure it was an accident. It happens all the time. People don't pay attention to motorcycles," he said after a few seconds. "You ready to get back on the bike, or shall I call a cab?" Jacks added with a chuckle.

"I'm good. Glad that didn't happen on the Tail of the Dragon!" Jennifer said, picking up her helmet.

Jacks moved to Jennifer before whispering, "You did good, baby. We would have gone down if you hadn't moved with me." He kissed her on the cheek.

"I said you were a great teacher. That proved my point." Jennifer said, brushing her lips over his. "Thanks for keeping me safe." Her brain was screaming to tell him she loved him, but her sensible side stopped her...again.

"As I was saying before our near-death experience," Jacks said, "our family is beginning a new tradition, Thanksgiving dinner at the beach, all my family will be there. Would you like to go?"

Meeting the parents—an uncomfortable feeling crept through her mind and body. She somehow found her voice and said, "Sounds like fun." Meeting his brothers was one thing, but his parents was another.

Chapter Eleven

Jennifer pushed the button on her steering wheel, "Hello there,"

"You survived the weekend?" Kimberly chuckled.

"Yes." She felt the heat rise into her face.

"Can you talk?"

"Sure, I'm at school waiting for the girls."

"How was it?"

"Wonderful." As the word crossed her lips, the warmth spread all over her body. Thoughts of Jacks' fingertips caressing her body caused her face to flush.

"Oh no, you don't. I want details. I saw the change between you and Jacks. At dinner, you couldn't keep your hands off each other."

"Good girls don't kiss and tell."

"You didn't let me off that easy after my first weekend with Brandon."

"I'll tell you when I see you. I promise," Jennifer said, checking her lipstick in the mirror.

"Pick the girls up and come for dinner. We'll have a scotch, and you can tell me everything. There's a crown roast on the grill, and there's plenty. The girls can do their homework in the office. I haven't seen them in weeks, plus we have puppies."

"Okay, we'll see you in about a half hour."

"I'll have the scotch waiting.

Jennifer turned on the radio and closed her eyes. She

118

was enjoying a replay of a shower with Jacks until a knock on her window caused her to jump. She turned to see Phillip. She pushed the button, and the glass slid down. "What?"

"Hello, good-looking."

"What are you doing here? Or better yet, what do you want?" She let the anger shout through in her calm words.

"I wanted to make sure you were here to get the girls."

"Of course, I'm here. Listen, I'm really not in the mood for three rounds of senseless conversation."

"You must have had a grand weekend."

Jennifer watched the girls enter the crosswalk. "Goodbye, Phillip," she said and rolled up the window. On purpose, she opened the door so fast, Phillip had to jump to avoid bring hit.

"How are my girls?" Jennifer said as she hugged them. It struck her she no longer had to bend down to embrace them. *Where have the years gone? How can they be fifteen?*

"Hi, Daddy. What are you doing here?" Morgan asked.

"I wanted to see you two and your mom."

"Cool," Madison added.

"Hug your father. We need to go," Jennifer said as she walked to the car.

The girls quickly said their goodbyes.

As they drove away, Jennifer said, "Kimberly and Brandon invited us to dinner. Does that work for you two?"

"It does for me," Madison answered.

"Me, too," Morgan added.

"Mom, did you have fun on your trip?"

"Very much, but I missed you two," Jennifer took a sip from her apple juice and returned the cup to the holder.

"Miss Lisa said you deserved to have a good time. She's happy you're dating," Morgan said.

"What?" Jennifer's head snapped to get a look at the girls in her rearview mirror.

"She and Daddy were talking. He said you were on a date," Madison added.

"Were you listening to an adult conversation?"

"No, we were walking by the room on the way to the pool," Madison added quickly.

In the review mirror, Jennifer saw Morgan punch Madison in the arm.

Before she could speak, Morgan asked, "Are you dating somebody, Mom?"

"It's nothing for you two to worry about." *Or was it?*

"We want to meet him," Morgan said timidly.

Madison chimed in with, "Is he cute? What's his name?"

Jennifer was speechless. "We'll talk about this later."

"Come on, Mom, we're fifteen. Daddy's married to Miss Lisa. Tell us, please?" Madison begged.

"We'll talk about this later."

"Bummer," came the response from the backseat.

She acted angry, but was smiling on the inside. Her daughters were growing up.

"When can we meet him?" Morgan asked.

"First of all, you shouldn't be listening to adult conversations, and you certainly couldn't have heard all that walking by an open door. I guess Jacks and I are dating. He's deploying right after Christmas. If I think things might get serious, I'll introduce you."

"What if you get serious, and we don't like him?" Morgan asked.

"You need somebody special, especially after what Daddy did," Madison said.

Jennifer made eye contact with Madison in the mirror and asked, "What do you mean by that?"

"Daddy told us he had to marry Miss Lisa," Madison answered.

"Girls, your father is a good man. He made some bad choices; it isn't all Lisa's fault."

"When do we get to meet Jacks?" Madison asked again.

Jennifer responded by turning up the radio.

****

Unfortunately for Jennifer, the third degree didn't stop when they arrived at Kimberly's house.

"Girls, it's good to see you. I've missed you," Kimberly said as she hugged the twins. "You can do your homework in the office. Make yourselves at home."

"We're almost done. We need to email our papers to the writing lab for review," Morgan said.

"Take care of your schoolwork, then we'll go see the new puppies"

The girl's faces lit up. "You have puppies?" Morgan asked.

"Yep. Last week the shelter called us to rescue a pregnant dachshund. Now we have six little babies."

"Cool!" With that, the girls were gone.

"Come on, spill it," Kimberly said, leaning on the counter, "You're beaming."

"What?" Jennifer rolled her eyes.

"You obviously rode more than the bike this weekend. How was it?"

"It was okay," Jennifer said as she opened the refrigerator and removed a pitcher of orange juice. "You saw the same things we did, colorful leaves, mountain views, and the like." She strolled around the kitchen island.

Kimberly placed two glasses on the island. "Thanks for the travel brochure. I want to know about the sex."

"Oh, that." Jennifer poured juice into each glass. "It was earth-moving, unbelievable, and fantastic."

"That's all I get?"

She stepped closer and whispered. "Kimberly, oh my lord. He's amazing. The man's packing quality equipment. And he's fully qualified to operate it."

"Do tell?" Kimberly said, licking her lips.

The response made Jennifer laugh. "We both enjoy being in control. Sometimes it was a very pleasant struggle until one of us gave in."

"Good for you. When are you going to see him again?"

"Not sure. He asked me to go away for Thanksgiving. Meet his parents."

"That's wonderful. Where?" Kimberly raised her glass and toasted Jennifer.

"The family beach house in Delaware."

"That's great. You'll love them."

Jennifer turned serious. "To change the topic completely, apparently, my weekend was discussed in great detail between Lisa and Phillip. The girls overheard a conversation about Jacks. Phillip was really pissed. He was at school Thursday morning, and our conversation turned ugly. He was there again this afternoon. It appears having a man in my life isn't sitting well. Now the girls want to meet Jacks."

"Introduce him," Kimberly said before taking a sip of her juice.

"He's leaving right after Christmas."

"Come on, think about it. What does it hurt for them to meet him? It's not like men are coming in and out of the house. You tell your girls the truth, and they know it. They're smart and level-headed teenagers. Besides, you're glowing like a thousand-watt bulb."

"I guess you're right."

"Good, because he's in the garage with Brandon. They're working on our motorcycle. Would you like to invite him to dinner, or should I?"

She was beaten. She felt the smile crawl on her face. Her heart pounded. "You can. It's your house."

Kimberly stood and headed toward the garage. The door opened before she reached it. "Hello, Kimberly. How's one of the most beautiful women I know?"

"You better not speak very loud. Jennifer's in the kitchen."

"Excuse me," he said as he stepped around Kimberly and headed toward the bar.

"Hi, gorgeous. This is a pleasant surprise."

Jennifer saw Kimberly's smile before Jacks lifted her chin and kissed her. "I didn't know you were coming over."

"Kimberly called while I was waiting for the girls at school."

"Are they here?" Jacks looked into the family room and around the kitchen.

"Yes. They want to meet you. By the way, we were

the topic of discussion this weekend. Are you okay with meeting them?"

"Of course. I want to."

Jennifer read happiness on his face.

As if right on cue, Morgan and Madison ran down the stairs. "Mom, we submitted our work. Can we see the puppies now?"

"Sure. Please come here first?"

"Yes, ma'am."

"Morgan and Madison, this is Mr. Williams. Jacks, these are my girls, Madison and Morgan."

"It's nice to meet you both. Now, how can I tell you apart?"

"Our rings. Morgan's is green and mine is blue. That's what most of our friends do," Madison added. Both held out their hands.

"I think Mom is the only one who can tell us apart. Even Dad and Miss Lisa have problems," Morgan said.

"Morgan, you play the violin and Madison the cello, right? Wait, I have that backward."

"That's okay. It's nice to meet you. We're going to see the dachshund puppies. Mr. Brandon said the next time he rescued puppies, we can help train them," Madison said as they both stepped forward and shook Jacks' hand.

"Hope to see you again soon," Morgan said.

When they were out of the room, Jacks said, "Wow, they're something else. Most fifteen-year-olds are in their own world. You're going to have problems soon."

"Thank you. But what problems?"

He stepped close to her, caressed her face, and said, "They are as beautiful as their mother. You'll have to chase the boys off with a stick."

She leaned in and kissed him.

He returned her kiss and slid his hands around her back, and whispered, "I want to take you upstairs and make love to you."

"It's only been two hours," she said. However, she was having the same thoughts. "Let's go see the puppies. I think the girls are going to hit me up for one each."

"You go ahead. I need a couple of minutes."

Jennifer couldn't stop herself from looking down at his jeans. She couldn't miss the bulge. When their eyes met, her wink didn't help his situation.

****

Jennifer watched the twins put their things in the car. Jacks pulled her into a small alcove. "There's something I want."

"What would that be, Commander Williams?"

"Let me show you." He backed her against the wall and covered her mouth with his. Slid a hand under her sweater, found an erect nipple, and stroked it. The kiss was full of hunger and desire. As quickly as it began, it was over. He stepped back and said, "Now you can go home."

She tried her best to appear angry. But a grin covered her face. She put her hands flat against his chest. "I'll see you tomorrow. I had a great time this weekend. "You better rest up. I have ten days off for Thanksgiving. Oh, but we won't be sleeping together at the beach."

"Thanks for that reminder. I can always creep down the hall after everyone's asleep."

"Goodbye, handsome." Jennifer kissed his cheek and strolled away.

****

The twins were quiet when their mom started the

car. The silence didn't last long, it began with giggling, and Morgan said, "Mom, Mr. Williams is cute and seems really nice. Do you think he was serious about the aquarium trip on Saturday?"

"Yes. He wouldn't have asked otherwise. Do you want to go? You don't have to spend time with him unless you want to."

"I want to," Madison replied quickly.

"Me, too," Morgan added.

"Okay, then we'll go. Perhaps we can pack a picnic."

Jennifer's panic grew again. What was she doing having Jacks meet the girls? Having them spend time together? He was only being nice. He was single. He would probably be glad when he deployed. This was a fling to him. Wasn't it? Jennifer's thought process was interrupted with the other question she thought she'd dodged.

"Mom, can we each have a dachshund from this litter? They're so cute," Madison asked.

Before she could answer, Morgan joined the conversation, "Mr. Brandon said he would help us house break them before they come home with us."

"Puppies are a great deal of work. What happens when we are gone all day? Or when you go to visit your father and Lisa?"

"Mr. Brandon said he'd help put in a dog door," Madison quickly added.

"I'm sure he did," Jennifer mumbled. "I'll talk to your father and Lisa. If they agree, the dogs can go with you during visits. I'll think about it."

"Okay." In response, a moan echoed from the back seat. Jennifer wasn't sure which one of the twins made the obnoxious sound. Maybe Phillip and Lisa would veto the puppies. That would save her from again being the heavy.

Chapter Twelve

Jacks met Jennifer at her house for lunch whenever possible. More often than not, food wasn't on the menu. "You, beautiful woman, are going to be my undoing," Jacks said as he began buttoning his uniform shirt.

"How's that, sailor?" Jennifer asked as she walked to him.

"All I think about is when I can see you again. This deployment's going to be a killer."

"I figured you'd welcome the rest. Are you sure you have to go back to work?" Jennifer asked as she began unbuttoning the tan buttons he'd already secured. "I'm doing paperwork from home this afternoon." She ran her hand inside his shirt and caressed his nipple.

"No. I have to go to work," he said as he stepped away and began buttoning his shirt again. "Put on some clothes, woman. You're driving me crazy," he said.

"As you wish," she said as she picked up the sheer robe she'd been wearing when he arrived. She tied the belt loosely so very little of her was covered.

"Thanks. But that's not helping."

She slowly ran her hands up his chest and around his neck. Pressed her body against his. She swayed against him in time to the classical music that floated around them. Her kiss sent him soaring. Immediately, his erection strained against his pants. She broke the kiss. "Now you can go back to work. That's payback for the other night at Brandon and Kimberly's." She laughed and let the robe drop.

"I'll get you back." He looked at his watch. "Not now, though. PT is in thirty minutes and today is a five-mile run."

"I could write Brandon a note explaining you've already had your workout for today."

"Thanks. I'm sure he'd love that. See you tomorrow at nine. I made a dinner reservation on the *Spirit of Norfolk.*"

"The girls will love it."

Jacks kissed his lover one more time and rushed to his car. He prayed traffic would be light. He arrived just in time to change for the run. Throughout the run, his thoughts were of his lover and their weekend. They'd made sweet love. Other times it had been hot, primal sex. He'd been with women who'd do one or the other. But Jennifer was different. He felt the warm satisfaction flow over him. Their weekend had been fun and serious. Jacks untied his shoelaces and slipped off his running shoes.

She was different about her divorce, too. She hadn't trashed her ex-husband. She'd shared how she quickly became pregnant, and perhaps he cheated because he felt trapped. When she'd lost the baby, he'd encouraged her to join the Air Force, go to college, and was supportive when she decided to take on postgraduate work. She'd even accepted part of the blame for their divorce. It had been ugly like his. He tossed his shoes and socks in his gym bag.

His thoughts drifted to her sitting at the bottom of the bed, crooking her finger for him to come to her. Which he'd eagerly done.

His thoughts were interrupted by the balance of the

squadron returning to the locker room. He removed his shirt.

"Williams, what wild cat got ahold of you?" One of his buddies teased.

"Wow, man, did you wrestle with a lioness?" Brandon added.

Jacks' mind went to one of their sexually charged sessions. Jennifer had clawed his back repeatedly as she climaxed. At the time it had been a turn-on, but now he'd let them have their fun. "Okay guys, let's say I fell into some bushes."

"That's the kind of bush I'd like to fall in," someone added from across the room.

Jacks replied with a hand gesture, wrapped a towel around his waist, and headed to the shower. They could tease all they wanted. But he'd be in Jennifer's arms as much as possible until the deployment. Jacks Williams was entranced.

****

"Hey, Mom," Jacks said after checking the caller id.

"Sorry to call so early. I know you usually sleep in on Sunday."

"I'm on the way to church."

After a pause, she added. "You're kidding, right?"

"No. Jennifer's girls are part of the youth worship service today, and they asked me to attend. They're direct and to the point, like their mother. Last weekend the four of us went to dinner on the *Spirit of Norfolk*. When Jennifer went to the restroom, Madison told me she was glad her mom had someone special in her life, and Morgan agreed."

"I'm happy for you. Y'all coming to the beach for Thanksgiving?"

"Yes, ma'am. We're excited about getting away."

"Wonderful. Your dad and I are looking forward to meeting Jennifer."

"Brandon asked if you and Dad are coming down for Christmas?"

"Wouldn't miss it."

"Great. When will you be here?"

"The twenty-first. If that works?"

"My leave starts on the nineteenth. Come down anytime. I'll let Jennifer and the girls know your plans."

"How old are the girls?"

"Sixteen in August."

"I hope we get to meet them."

"I'm sure you will. Gotta go, Mom. I'm at the church. Wish me luck. I'm meeting the ex-husband and his wife today."

"It should be an interesting service," Jacks' mother said with a chuckle.

"Love you, Mom. Hello to Dad."

****

Jacks scanned the sanctuary for Jennifer, and a smile grew on his face. She was wearing red again, combined with high heels that showed off her sexy legs. Her hair flowed down her back, held in place by a gold and pearl clip. A gift he'd given her last week.

"Good to have you with us," Pastor Bell said as they shook hands. "You picked a great day to visit. The youth are in charge of the service."

"I know. Morgan and Madison Ryan invited me."

"Great girls, I hope to see you after worship," the pastor said, stepping to the side.

"Thanks," Jacks said.

Three more people greeted Jacks before he reached

Jennifer.

"Morning, beautiful," Jacks said. He loved the way her eyes lit up when she saw him.

"Hey."

"Mr. Jacks, you came," Morgan said. "Madison, Mr. Jacks is here."

"Cool beans. Hi." Without taking a breath, Madison said to her sister, "We need to get our robes."

"Mom, Mr. Jacks, we'll see you after the service," Morgan added.

"I'll be right here in the front row," Jacks said.

Madison stepped to him and whispered, "Presbyterians never sit on the front row. You can ask Mom why." Her grin was infectious.

"Okay. We'll be on the second row."

"Awesome," Madison added as a parting comment.

"You want to sit?" Jennifer suggested and took his hand.

"That would be wonderful. But first, why don't Presbyterians sit on the front row?"

"Who told you that?" Jennifer inquired.

"Madison said you'd explain."

Her smile blossomed as she lowered her voice and spoke, "It's an old joke. The Presbyterian line is, let me write my check for ten percent, and don't make me sit on the front row. In other words, let me meet my tithe and stay out of the limelight."

"My parents never told me that one. They're Presbyterian, too."

"Small world, I guess. What are you grinning about?" she whispered.

He stepped close and replied in a tone only she could hear. "Nothing, you look incredibly sexy in that dress."

"You clean up pretty nice yourself." She adjusted his tie. "Are you wearing cuff links?"

"Yep. Pull them out occasionally."

"Can I see?"

"Sure." Jacks held out his wrist.

Jennifer ran her fingers over the silver insignia. "I can make out an eagle and the anchor. What is the other?"

"A flintlock pistol."

"It's beautiful. Oh, I read your father's biography. He was a SEAL, too. He must be very proud of you."

"Well, you can believe most of the life and times of the old man, but you'll see another side of him at Thanksgiving." Jacks grinned and straightened his cufflink. "The eagles always face forward."

He took her hand, and the pair stood in silence. He wanted to say I love you. But the words wouldn't come.

Jennifer exhaled a long sigh of contentment.

"Me too," he whispered as a wave of joy flowed through him. They were enclosed in a cocoon of happiness.

Jennifer was the first to speak. "I guess we need to head to the sanctuary."

"Lead on," Jacks said and placed his hand in the small of her back. He fought to control the emotions assaulting his body.

Lisa was already seated. "Hey, Jennifer, Phillip's parking the car.

"Lisa, this is Jacks Williams,"

"Nice to meet you. The girls are still raving about the trip to the aquarium and the dinner cruise."

"I have a friend at the aquarium. They got the insider's tour. I'm glad they had a good time."

Lisa was about to respond when Phillip arrived. "You must be the amazing Jacks Williams," he said as Jacks stood to shake his hand.

"Guilty as charged, I guess."

"*My* girls told us about their wonderful weekend with you and Jennifer."

"I was telling Lisa I have a friend at the aquarium. It was a great outing. Everyone seemed to enjoy the day."

"I'm sure they did. I prefer you didn't spoil my children."

"Let's sit. The service is about to begin," Jennifer said.

Jacks felt pride in how Jennifer defused Phillip's escalating hostility. He enjoyed the service. The music was exceptional.

As the service ended, the twins hurried to the pew.

"Hey, Daddy, I'm so glad you and Miss Lisa came," Morgan said as both girls hugged them.

"Mr. Jacks, did you enjoy the service?" Madison asked.

"Yes, very much. You ladies are extremely talented. I'm going to guess the musical piece was "Adagio Affettuoso Ed Appassionato," by Beethoven."

"Correct. The title was wrong in the bulletin. You know about classical music?" Madison asked.

"Somewhat."

"Let's head to the fellowship hall for coffee?" Phillip suggested.

"Okay. We'll meet you there after we pack our instruments," Morgan said.

"I'll take care of the instruments. We'll meet you in the fellowship hall," Jennifer said.

"Thanks, Mom. See you in a few," Madison said.

Jacks and Jennifer placed the instruments in the cases and collected the music. "I don't think Phillip was happy to see me. I hope my being here won't cause a problem," Jacks said as they walked to the car.

"No. The problem is Phillip doesn't want anyone in my life except him. The girls and I are happy you came. Don't worry about him. You, my love, are a triple threat. You outrank him, are much sexier, and you're my lover. He has to accept it and move on."

"My ego just received a huge boost," Jacks said. He brushed his lips against hers. He was surprised when she responded with a passionate kiss.

He smiled and shifted gears in an attempt to stop his skyrocketing libido. "Let's get inside before I pull you into the backseat."

The girls were at their mother's side the minute she entered the room. "Mom, can Daddy and Miss Lisa come with us to lunch?" Morgan asked, but both girls' eyes danced with excitement.

"I'll talk to him in a minute."

"Cool."

Jennifer turned to Jacks. "Do you mind if they join us? I don't want to make you feel uncomfortable."

"It's fine. Besides, I'll take guilty pleasure watching Phillip stew." He lowered his voice and continued, "If the shoe was on the other foot, the thought of another man making love to you would drive me insane." His smile widened before he continued, "Or I could thank him for all the little tricks he taught you." Jennifer began to blush.

"I never should have told you that about Phillip. I'll be right back."

As the beautiful woman crossed the room, Jacks let

out the breath he didn't realized he'd been holding. He was in trouble. Jennifer was different than anyone he'd met. He was falling for her; hell, he was already gone. The approaching trio pulled him from the somewhat disturbing realization.

"Okay, we're ready. They're going to meet us at the Officer's Club. Morgan, you and your sister riding with your dad?"

"Can we ride in Mr. Jacks' car? It's super cool, please?" Madison asked.

She picked up on Jacks' quick nod. "Sure. We'll pick up my car later."

Jacks took Jennifer's hand as they headed to the exit. Yep, he was in big trouble. The question was what he would do about it. For now, file the feeling away. That was it.

****

Jacks stretched, and grabbed his watch from the nightstand. He stroked Jennifer's back. "Hey, sleepy head, it's time to get up. The girls will be home soon."

Jennifer rolled on her side, propped her head on her hand, and looked into his eyes. "You were the one that suggested we come to my place for a nap after lunch. I don't want to get out of bed. Perhaps I could persuade you to stay."

He smiled at the gorgeous woman, her curls in disarray. He could muss her hair a bit more.

"I'm sure you could very easily entice me to make love to you again. But you already have the look—how shall I put this delicately—like you've spent the afternoon in bed and not sleeping."

"Okay, killjoy, you're saying I look like a woman who's been—how shall I put this delicately—completely satisfied?" she asked, climbing from the four-poster bed. She slipped into a red bra and panties and removed a pair of jeans and a T-shirt from the dresser.

"Do you have those in every color?"

"What, the jeans?" she asked with a chuckle.

"No, the underthings." Jacks licked his lips. Perhaps he'd take her back to bed after all.

"Yep. I bought several after the divorce. The only time I wear white is under my dress uniform. When I wear my operational camouflage uniform or civilian clothing, it's all color all the time."

"Thanks for the picture. Now I'll always wonder what color you're wearing. Would they be something you'd like as a gift?"

"Sure, but you have to guess the size."

"I bet I can make you tell me."

He was across the room in six steps and began an all-out assault on her neck and lips. "Now, will you tell me?"

"No, but keep that up, and I might."

When she began to giggle, he stopped. "I may be wounded forever."

Jennifer placed her palms on his chest and pushed. "Okay, okay, the panties are a six and the bra is a 36C. Now get dressed before I seduce you again.

Chapter Thirteen

"Did you guys have a good time?" Jennifer asked as the group entered the house.

"It was awesome. You should see Miss Lisa skate," Madison said.

"Is that so? How did you do?" Jennifer asked both girls.

"Better than last time. I made it around the rink twice without falling. Where's Mr. Jacks?" Morgan asked, looking around her mother.

"I'm right here. I was putting chicken on the grill. Your mom's letting me cook," he said, entering the kitchen. Did you have a good time?"

"Sure did," Morgan said.

"It was great, and Morgan's boyfriend was there," Madison teased.

"Madison, shut up," Morgan said, punching her sister in the arm.

"Ouch," she responded with a punch.

"All right, you two, put your coats away. Would you like something to drink?" Jennifer asked Lisa and Phillip.

She saw Lisa look to Phillip for an answer, "Sure, if it isn't too much trouble."

Jennifer stopped in front of the coffee bar. "I have Russian tea mix I make every year."

"That works," Phillip said.

138

"How about you, Lisa?"

"I'll try the tea, thank you."

As they enjoyed the drinks, Jennifer made a salad, and the twins set the table.

Phillip asked, "Jacks, what ship are you attached to?"

"The *GW*, the *George Washington.*"

"When do you deploy?"

"A firm date hasn't been set."

Jennifer watched the men. She could read Phillip like an old familiar novel. He was sizing Jacks up and didn't like what he saw. Jacks seemed to be claiming his status with very little effort. Her ex appeared to be getting more aggravated as the minutes ticked by. For some reason, that caused her to smile...on the inside anyway.

"Sweetheart, how long before the chicken will be ready?" Jennifer asked.

"About ten minutes."

"We better go," Phillip said, his aggravation clear to everyone in the room.

"Girls, tell your dad and Lisa goodbye. Wash your hands for dinner."

"Yes, ma'am."

Alone moments later, Jacks said, "Phillip doesn't like me. I think he's going to be trouble when I deploy."

She was about to answer when the girls returned. "Mom, did you make sweet potato balls?"

"I certainly did. Fix a salad. The chicken is sliced. The dressings and stuff are on the table. I'll bring in the potatoes."

****

Jacks dried the large glass bowl and placed it on the

counter. He felt at home here. He'd miss all three of his ladies when he deployed. *His ladies.* That thought caught him off guard. It had only been a few weeks, and he was very happy with them in this life.

"You're very quiet," Jennifer said, loading the dishwasher.

Jacks dried his hands. "Thinking about the deployment. It's going to be tough to say goodbye. Could you meet me in Rota, Spain? You can bring the girls," he quickly added.

Jennifer slipped her hands around his neck. "Would you be disappointed if I came alone?"

"No. I want you to know the girls are important, too." He pulled her tight against him. "Damn, I'm going to miss you." His feeling roused old fears and uncertainties from his marriage. Would Jennifer grow tired of waiting? No. She wasn't like that.

"Look at me," Jennifer whispered. Her eyes were gentle and contemplative. As if she read his thoughts. "When we started seeing each other, we said we'd take it one day at a time. Of course, I'll meet you in Rota. I'll be here when you come home. We'll figure the rest out along the way. Okay?"

The knot in his stomach relaxed a bit. "Okay."

Jacks looked over her shoulder through the bay window. "Wow, snow before Thanksgiving. "Is this normal?"

"Not really. The weather forecast was twenty percent chance of snow. It'll quickly turn into rain. Does it snow in Delaware during Thanksgiving?"

"It has a couple of times. I haven't been there enough to have a point of reference, though." The lightness of the conversation lifted his spirits. "Are you ready for the trip?"

"I've never been to Slaughter's Beach or Delaware, for that matter. How far is the drive?"

"About three hours with stops."

"Wonderful. I love the beach in the wintertime," Jennifer said and led him to the couch.

"It's my favorite time, too. But I'm not surprised by that at all." Jacks gently kissed her lips. He broke the contact when his phone rang. "Hold that thought, sexy."

"Hey, man. It's Hollister at The Raven."

"What's up?"

"Troy's here. Drinking and itching for a fight."

"I'll be there in twenty," Jacks said and ended the call.

"What's up?" Jennifer asked.

"Troy's at The Raven. That was Hollister, the bartender. He wants me to come get him. I'm not sure I'll be back."

"Should I come?"

"Probably not. I'll call if there's a problem."

"Okay." She kissed Jacks on the cheek.

****

Jacks scanned the Raven Bar and made eye contact with Hollister. The pair acknowledged each other with a simple nod. The bartender motioned toward the end of the bar with his eyes.

Troy was sitting on a stool, staring into his glass. His shoulders hunched. Chin in his hand.

Jacks gave Hollister another nod. By the time he sat next to Troy, there was a shot of whiskey waiting. "Hey, brother."

"Hey," Troy replied without raising his head. His voice was fragile and shaky.

"You want to grab some dinner?"

"Nope. I want to be alone and drink until I'm ready to stop. And that won't be any time soon."

"Okay. I'll join you." Jacks drained his glass and signaled for another round.

"Did you miss the 'I want to be alone' part?" Troy turned his head slightly and glared.

Jacks read his friend's pain. This was more than the mission that had taken his arm and most of his sanity. "Lucky for you, I don't listen very well."

"Hear this, brother, leave me alone, or I'll kick your ass six ways to Sunday," he said and turned the empty glass over on the bar.

"I'm not leaving. I don't think you could stand up long enough to kick anything, much less my ass. But if that's what you need, let's take it outside. We'll go best two out of three."

Troy huffed. "Don't want to fight you. Leave me alone, okay?" he said and threw back another shot.

"Not an option. What's going on?"

"Nothing, I need to get drunk," he said in a grudging voice. A bit louder this time.

"Your old lady back?" Jacks asked.

"So, you fuckin' Doc regular? Figured she'd be a high-class great piece of ass. Maybe when you ship out, you'd put in a good word for me. I'd love to tap some of that."

Jacks saw red, threw a fifty on the counter, pulled Troy off his stool, dragged him out of the bar and into the alley. He shoved his friend against the brick wall, his face inches from Troy's and yelled "Don't talk about her that way! She not a piece of ass, you hear me? Say it again and I'll kick yours!" Jacks dodged the first swing before it connected.

"That's what all women are, whores. Don't you get it?" Troy shouted and shoved Jacks backward. "Leave me alone. Go back to your slut."

"That's it." Jacks swung and connected with Troy's jaw. "I said don't talk about her like that."

Troy got in a hit to Jacks' abdomen.

Jacks planted his fist against Troy's jaw again.

"All right, you two, break it up," Hollister yelled as two men pulled them apart. "The cops are on the way. Virginia Beach's finest don't play."

"Put him in my car. I'll take him home. We'll get his truck tomorrow. Troy can sleep it off on my sofa," Jacks said as he tucked in his shirt.

"I didn't mean that about Doc. It was a cheap shot," Troy mumbled from the passenger seat.

"We're good, brother," Jacks said.

****

"Hello sweetie, thanks for the lilies. I love all the different shades of purple, and they smell amazing," Jennifer said.

"I wish I could say you're welcome, but I didn't send you flowers. They must be from your other lover." She picked up a trace of laughter in his voice.

"Stop kidding around." Her stomach churned, and her voice quivered as she spoke.

"Baby, I'm not. I didn't send you lilies. Where are you?"

"Home," she murmured.

"Where were the flowers?"

"On the front porch in a box," she answered and sat on the stairs.

"It appears you have a secret admirer."

"If you didn't send them, it's no secret who they're from."

"He's persistent. I give him that. I'll be there in twenty."

"Okay, see you then." She crammed the box in the trash can and slammed the lid. She started to dial Phillip, but that would give him exactly what he wanted, her attention. She shoved the phone in her pocket.

****

"Is it finished? Can I look?" Jennifer asked, biting her bottom lip. She'd been unable to watch Jacks and Brandon cut a rectangle in her antique kitchen door. Instead, she'd paced around the house. She kept reminding herself they knew what they were doing. Why was she hiding around the corner in her own house?

"Come on. Check it out," Jacks said with a laugh. As she entered the kitchen, he stood and brushed his hands together.

"Wow. It looks great."

"Don't sound so surprised. We weren't exactly doing a major renovation." Brandon said before sipping his coffee.

"Sorry. You know how much trouble I had finding the antique door. Plus, all the time I spent sanding it back to the original wood."

"Baby, your door is fine. It's the only place we could have put a dog door," Jacks said. He moved behind her and put his hands on her shoulders. The simple act spoke volumes and shot a feeling of happiness through her body.

"We could have put in another door or cut through the wall," Brandon added as he moved the cup to his lips and emptied it.

"Stop, both of you." Jennifer placed her hand over Jacks'. "Thank you both so very much. The girls are going to be speechless."

"We'll see how long it takes them to notice the door," Jacks replied.

"Call me when you guys are heading over," Brandon said over his shoulder as he headed for the front door.

Jennifer and Jacks followed behind him. "See you in a couple of hours."

Brandon stopped and turned around. "I was supposed to ask you guys to stay for dinner after the grand puppy selection process."

Jennifer stepped toward her friend, stood on her tiptoes, kissed him on the cheek, and whispered, "You are a wonderful friend. Thanks for all the help, I mean with everything." She moved from his arms and fought back the tears in her eyes.

He placed his fingers on Jennifer's chin, smiled down at her, and winked. "I'm glad you're my friend, too."

Jennifer waved until Brandon was in his car. She was so blessed to have a great circle of friends she could rely on. Suddenly a feeling of complete happiness soaked into her body. It was an awakening experience that left her senses reeling.

"I'm not sure what you're smiling about, but I hope it's me," Jacks said when she turned.

Jennifer paused. "I had an epiphany," she said, stepping to him.

"And what would that be?" Jacks whispered in her ear after he pulled her tight against him.

Jennifer rested her head on his chest and listened to his heartbeat. She sighed before continuing, "I'm happy, really happy. I'm not sure when the shift happened. I was hurt and confused. Felt like I would never be happy again. But *poof,* here I am."

Jacks kissed Jennifer on the top of the head. "You want to go for a walk by the water?"

"Maybe, in a minute, this feels nice." What she really wanted to say was *I love you.* But the words wouldn't come.

****

Jennifer and Jacks heard Morgan squeal from the kitchen, "Madison, we have a dog door!"

"Didn't take long for them to find the door." Jacks stood and helped Jennifer up from the sofa.

"Mom?" Morgan yelled as she ran toward her. "Does this mean we can get a puppy?"

"Yes," Jennifer said as both girls hugged her.

"One puppy for us to share or one dachshund each?" Madison asked.

"You each get to pick a puppy. Remember, they're your dogs, and you must take care of them. Perhaps starting with one might be better."

Jennifer watched her daughters stop jumping and give her their best pouts. "We'll take care of them, we promise, right, Morgan?" Madison asked.

"Yep. Thanks, Mom, you're the best." Morgan said before both girls grabbed their phones and began texting their friends.

Morgan stopped in mid-text. Smiled at her mother and asked, "Wait, when do we get to go?"

"As soon as you're ready," Jennifer said.

Phones forgotten, the girls scurried to the kitchen bench to put on their shoes.

"Well, looks like we're headed to Kimberly's. You

want to join us?" Jennifer asked. She wanted him to say yes, to be part of this special time in the lives of her girls.

Jacks turned to Jennifer and placed his forehead on hers. Kissed her nose and whispered, "Are you kidding? I wouldn't miss this for the world."

His smile was infectious. Jennifer placed her head on his chest. He closed her in his arms. She listened to his heartbeat and pushed back the tears of happiness. "Jacks, I'm going to miss this. I'm so happy."

Jacks kissed Jennifer on the top of her head.

"You guys ready or what?" Madison asked.

Jennifer was saved when her girls came around the corner. The words "I love you" were bubbling up from her soul.

Jacks stepped back, winked. "Me too, baby" he mouthed.

Jennifer tingled all over. He felt the same. This would all be fine. Damn, she was already counting the days until he left. Dreading as each one passed.

****

Jennifer barely had the car in park before Madison and Morgan were out of the car. She watched as they bypassed the house and headed straight to the shop.

"Here we go. I guess the next step will be a shopping spree at our local pet shop," Jennifer was saying when Kimberly opened the door.

"Hey, you two, come on in," Kimberly said, stepping aside. "Where are the twins?"

"They're already in the shop. I'm not sure I've ever seen them this happy," Jennifer said as she hugged her friend.

"Hey, handsome," Kimberly said, hugging Jacks.

"Hey there," Jacks replied.

"Brandon's in the shop. You guys want something to drink before we head out?"

"I'm good. Jacks?" Jennifer asked.

"Nope, I'm good. The girls are bursting at the seams to select a puppy."

"I think they've already decided. Brandon says they've been playing with the same ones every time they come over," Kimberly said, opening the back door.

****

Jacks leaned against the wall; everyone was having a good time. Madison selected a female black-and-silver wire hair. Morgan's choice was a short-haired red smooth little girl. The puppies wiggled as Brandon slipped a small ribbon on each of the girl's choices.

As Jennifer wiped her eyes, Jacks pushed away from the wall and joined her. "Cutie, you, okay?" he asked as she snapped a picture.

"Yes. They're so grown up, I'm not sure where the time has gone."

Jacks took her hand. "You've done an incredible job. They're great kids."

"Thanks. I love them so much. Soon they'll be gone to college."

"When they leave, you can be the crazy dachshund lady."

"Oh, don't remind me. I'm already trying to wrap my head around the fact the girls will leave for college soon enough. At least the dogs will keep me company. I have a feeling once the girls leave, the house is going to be really quiet." *Unless you're there,* crept into Jennifer's mind.

"Where are they looking to go to college?"

"Harvard is their first choice, I think."

"You know, my parents went there, so did Max and Alex," Jacks said, taking her hand.

"Yes. Adams Wallingford, Lisa's father, and Lisa graduated from there, too."

"Sounds like they'll be a shoe-in."

"Their grades and extra-curricular activities are in check; they start applying in January."

Jacks was about to respond when Madison joined them.

"Isn't she the cutest thing ever?" she said, holding the small ball of hair toward her mother.

"Well, next to mine," Morgan interrupted, snuggling the red dachshund.

"You have names picked out?" Jacks asked as he petted the small dogs.

"I'm thinking about Kandi," Morgan responded with a shrug.

"Hazel or maybe Olivia from Shakespeare, from the countess in *The Twelfth Night,*" Madison added and went back to cuddling her new baby.

"You have a couple of weeks to decide," Jennifer said, snapping pictures of the new additions to the family.

Chapter Fourteen

Jennifer leaned back against the footboard and surveyed the man in her bed, Jacks slept on his stomach, dead center of the mattress. His arms spread under the pillow. He took up almost the entire bed. A sheet was draped across his butt and lower thighs.

She could feel her desire rising. The sight of his back and arm muscles was certainly sexy—the arms that had held her tight and rippled when he was poised above her.

She used her toes to slowly pull the sheet off his body. He stirred a bit. She crawled up the bed like a tiger stalking its prey. She reached his torso, straddled him, and placed small kisses across his shoulder blade.

"Umm." Jacks murmured, lifted his shoulders, and turned enough to see her. "Good morning, sexy."

"Hello," she replied and massaged his shoulder muscles.

"You can do that all day. It's amazing."

"I love your tattoo. The colors are vibrant. The shading makes it look like the flag is raised. Where did you get it done?" she asked and ran her nails down his arms until her breasts were flat against his back.

"Norfolk. About six years ago. Oh yeah, that feels awesome."

"Were you stationed here before?" Jennifer asked, and then placed kisses on his neck.

"Nope, I was here on temporary duty."

"How did you choose this design?" Jennifer asked as she continued what she wanted to be a rewarding end to her foreplay.

Jacks purred before he answered. "The guy at the ink shop talked to me and designed it. Do you want a tat? One would look amazing on your ass." He reached back and ran his fingers up her thigh.

"I've thought about it several times but never went through with it."

"Then let's do it. I'll call my connection after breakfast. You keep touching me like that, and it'll be after lunch."

"We'll see," Jennifer replied and asked, "Did you sleep well?"

"Some, but I seemed to have had a reoccurring problem."

"What's that?" Jennifer asked, running her hands down his arms and up his sides.

"You."

"Did I take up too much of the bed?"

"No." He shook his head.

"Snore?"

"Nope."

"What did I do?"

"You kept me wanting more of you, like now."

"I was going to start the coffee," she said.

He rose on his arms and legs like she wasn't even there, reached back with his right hand, leaned left, and in a blink, she was on her back facing him.

"I get the idea there's something you want more," he whispered, nuzzling her neck.

Jennifer ran her nails down his back. "I certainly do."

"Just name it."

"I think you are on the right path."

Jacks slid his knee between her thighs. "I kept dreaming about doing this," he took her left nipple between his lips. His tongue whipped around the hard bud and nibbled with his teeth.

Jennifer began to squirm beneath him as he switched to sucking. "Is that all you dreamed about?" she asked and stroked his neck with her fingertips.

"Oh no. I'm just getting started." Jacks kissed his way down her stomach. He moved her thighs apart and stroked her with his index finger. Soon she was moving against him.

"You could drive a man mad," Jacks demanded and drove his full length inside her.

"Oh, Jacks," Jennifer yelled as an orgasm bolted through her.

"Christ, Jennifer, you're hot as hell, so wet and hot," Jacks' voice was rough and raspy.

"Yes, oh, yes, please don't stop. It feels so good," Jennifer whispered in his ear before they both flew into the storm of pleasure.

****

Jennifer stepped through the tattoo shop door. Brandon and Jacks followed her.

"Brandon, how are ya?" Mark asked as the pair shook hands.

"Good, brother, you?"

"It's all good."

"Jacks, good to see you." The two men exchanged handshakes.

"Same here. This is Jennifer." The tall, lean man was covered in tats. His long hair in a ponytail.

"Nice to meet you," he said as he took her hand. "I gather the tattoos I've been designing are for you?"

"Yes." She smiled to hide her nervousness.

He led her to a small table. "Come on back. Let's see if you like one of my designs. Have a seat. Would you like a coffee or water?"

"No. I'm okay."

Mark placed a folder on the table and sat across from her. He seemed to be staring.

Jennifer smiled. "What?" she finally asked with a giggle.

"My designs are all wrong." He pitched the file in the trash. "Give me a minute." He removed a sheet of paper from a bin and began to sketch.

Jacks stood behind Jennifer, his hands on her shoulders.

She watched as the outline of an open rose took shape. He added a stem and four dainty leaves. She was fascinated as he colored in the bright yellow and shaded it with others. The design seemed to jump off the page.

He worked like a man possessed. When he turned the sheet around, she couldn't speak, it was so beautiful. Two small multi-colored hummingbirds hovered over a rose, and a vine extended about two inches to each side. It was a masterpiece. The birds were colored in shades from lavender to amethyst.

"Do you like?" Mark asked.

"Yes. Very much."

"Sorry, do you want to see the others I drew?" he asked almost as an afterthought.

She smiled and shook her head. "This is perfect."

"I'll get the paperwork."

Jacks walked around and sat down in front of her.

"It's your eyes. I told you they're magical."

"Right," she said with a laugh.

Mark placed paperwork in front of her and said, "If you'll fill in this form. We'll get started. I'm going to lock the front door. You're my last client."

Paperwork done; Jennifer sat on the table in a small room. It reminded her of a doctor's office, except for the pictures of tats covering the wall.

"There's a tradition here," Jacks said, setting a bottle of Patron, salt, and a bowl of lime slices on the desk. "You're becoming part of a very small special group. Mark will do your tattoo and burn the design in front of you. He'll never use it again."

"Okay," Jennifer said, a bit anxious. "I thought you weren't supposed to drink before getting a tattoo."

"Well, there is that school of thought. It's more so people don't get tanked and get a tat they will regret. Trust me?"

"Yes," she tentatively replied. But doubt still lingered. "I'm good," she said a bit more confidently.

"Outstanding. Ever done tequila shots before?"

"No." She shook her head.

"Would you like to?"

After a brief pause, she shrugged her shoulders and said, "Why not? Who am I to argue with tradition?"

"We ready?" Brandon asked as Mark entered the room with shot glasses.

"Sure," Jennifer said, taking a deep breath.

"Okay, sweetie. Lick your hand. It's really easier to show you."

Mark broke the seal on the bottle of Gran Patron Platinum and poured the liquid into three shot glasses. Jennifer watched the men lick their hands between their thumb and forefinger, sprinkle salt in the area. Lick it again, bite the lime, and swallow the entire shot.

"You ready?"

"I guess."

The tequila felt like fire in her throat; she fought the urge to cough.

All three men laughed. "You okay?" Mark asked.

"Sure, I may never breathe again, but I'm okay."

"You're one behind us," he said with a laugh. And set up another round for the three of them. "One, two, three, go."

After the third shot Jennifer felt warm all over and had an amazing buzz. She lay on the table trying to focus. "Hey, beautiful," Jacks whispered.

"Hey yourself. You got me drunk."

"I sure did. It'll make things a bit easier for you."

"If you say so."

He kissed her hand. "There's a better way to do shots."

"Really?"

He leaned and whispered, "I can lick the salt anyplace off your body."

"Or I can lick it off yours, right?"

Jacks let out a long slow breath. "You certainly can."

"You ready," Mark asked.

"I think so." Jennifer's words slurred.

"Good. Roll over on your stomach."

Jennifer followed his directions to expose her lower back. Mark rubbed her back with a warm solution and began his work.

Jennifer promptly went to sleep.

Brandon took another shot. "Damn, that woman is

something else."

"She certainly is, and gentleman, she's all mine," Jacks said. "Pour me one more."

****

Jennifer buttoned the fly of her jeans. The extra mile she and Kimberly added to their run, and the increased weightlifting had produced a five-pound loss. She was under her pre-pregnancy weight. She wondered what Jacks would say when he discovered the black sheer bra and panties underneath her outfit.

The hip-hugger jeans were low, but she'd grown accustomed to them. As she left the bathroom, she turned and looked over her shoulder into the full-length mirror. The top of the yellow rose and hummingbird tat was visible. She had to look close to see the tiny SEAL trident in the design and Mark's initials. She slipped into a Harley Davidson Key West T-shirt, it covered the picture, but Jacks would have brief glimpses when she moved.

She picked up her boots and headed downstairs. There was enough time for a second cup of coffee before Jacks arrived. Soon they'd be headed up the eastern shore on his bike.

The coffee mug felt warm in her hands. She worked her way around the kitchen, putting things into their proper place. She heard the front door open and close.

"Mom, it's us," Madison said from the hall.

"I'm in the kitchen."

Jennifer hugged her daughter. "Hey, Mom."

"Hey back. You forget something?"

"Morning, Mom," Morgan said as she joined her sister in the kitchen "Cool T-shirt."

"Thanks."

"We both forgot our chemistry books. There's a test on Monday."

"Is Lisa with you?"

"No. She stayed at home," Phillip said as he strolled into the kitchen. His hands in the pockets of his pressed tan trousers; his yellow golf shirt accented his tan.

"Phillip. You should've called. You can't just stop by.

"I didn't think you'd mind." He leaned against the island.

The smug look on his face made Jennifer want to slap him. She dug deep for the strength to remain calm. "That's not the point. Girls, go grab your books."

Phillip flashed a smile. "I didn't interrupt anything, did I?" He paused, looking around. "How about a cup of coffee for your husband?"

"Ex-husband," she responded with a great deal of disdain, hoping Phillip would catch her annoyance.

"You've lost weight."

"I've stepped up my workout routine." She turned, opened the cabinet, and reached for a cardboard to-go cup.

"What the hell! You have a damn tramp stamp on your back!" Phillip shouted.

Jennifer caught his contemptuous tone sparked with anger. But she didn't miss a beat. "I have a tattoo, if that's what you're referring to. She poured coffee into the cup and snapped the plastic lip in place.

Phillip paced the kitchen. "Have you lost your mind? You're a mother of teenagers, for heaven's sake. What the hell are you doing wearing hip-huggers and getting tattoos? That damn naval aviator forced you to. Didn't he?" He stepped within inches and glared into her eyes.

She grinned and bit her lip, "I'm having a wonderful time. You got what you wanted, and so have I. I love being single. I had no idea how much fun life can be."

"You're trying to make me jealous." He ran his hand down her cheek. When she pulled away, he continued, "All you need do is ask. I'll be yours as often as you like; Lisa would be none the wiser. You don't need a sailor to make you do things you don't want to, like getting a stupid tattoo. He's using you as a handy piece of ass until he ships out. No man will ever make you feel the way I do; I know every inch of your body and how to please you," he said reaching to her again.

This time she laughed, but it wasn't one of pleasure. She stepped into his personal space, locked eyes, and lowered her voice, "Trying to make you jealous, really? Is that what you think?" All the years of anger and hurt she'd kept buried rose to the surface. "I love my life. I'm happier than I've ever been."

"You really expect me to believe that, the way you fought the divorce?"

This time she smiled for real. "Did you really think I'd be your whore? Take you into my bed behind Lisa's back? Be the other woman? I have more self-respect than that, and I certainly deserve a man who understands the concept. Are you really that stupid? Wake up. I held out for the divorce only until I knew you'd give into all my demands."

"Bullshit, you fought me tooth and nail," Phillip said as he leaned back against the center island, crossing his arms.

Jennifer shook her head and smiled. "I held out until I knew you were desperate because of Lisa's condition.

My plan B worked quite well. I got everything, even you into my bed for one last show."

"That's not true. It's that damn sailor talking."

"Well, yes, now that you bring him up. Thanks to him, I understand what you meant about the difference between making love and having sex. He does things to me you wish I'd let you try." Her contemptuous tone roared with anger. "Jacks pleases me all night, not once the way he wants it, then rolls over and goes to sleep. We have mind-blowing sex."

"Is that so?"

Phillip tried to play it off, but his tone told her she'd hit him where it hurt. "You might want to move your hand from the counter. We had sex there last night. He couldn't get my leathers and jeans off quick enough. I was lucky we even got in the house. Hear this," She poked him in the chest. "I don't want or need you in my house or my bed. If Jacks is using me, then thank the stars above. Do we understand each other?"

Phillip stared at her with his eyes wide.

"Call me the next time you decide to drop in." She pasted a smile on her face as the girls returned to the kitchen. "Come give me goodbye hugs," Jennifer said, opening her arms. "Now put your things in the car. Your father will be right out."

In a calm, steady soft voice, she said, "Phillip, this is *my life*. No man will ever again tell me what to do. It's my body, my choice." She shoved the cup into his chest. "Now take your coffee and get out."

Phillip left without a word.

Jennifer paced around the kitchen, fuming. *How dare that lousy son of a bitch think I would try to make him jealous? Of all the narcissistic ideas—I'd want him back? All right, Jennifer, stop and think like a psychologist for a second. He was trying to pick a fight, ruin your day. Don't let him win.* She walked through the sunroom and down the path to the bay.

Chapter Fifteen

Jacks found Jennifer drinking coffee and gazing over the water. "Hey, sexy," he said and placed his hands on her shoulders and immediately felt the knots. She dropped the cup and turned.

"Hey, baby." Immediately her red, swollen eyes pulled him in. She put her head on his chest. He closed his arms around her. He'd learned to give her time, and she'd talk if she needed. And he was right.

She stepped back and said, "The girls both forgot their chemistry books. Phillip brought them by. We had words; I lost my temper."

He scanned her face. "Did you say anything you didn't mean?"

"No." She shook her head.

Because she didn't continue this time, he asked, "And?"

"You'll get pissed off."

"So? Tell me. I detect the beginnings of a grin. I'd like to take credit, but I think you did this all on your own."

"He saw my tattoo, called it a tramp stamp. Said I was trying to make him jealous, and you were using me until you deploy."

"That lousy—"

Put her hands on his chest. "Wait, listen, I told him about the other night, how I turned you on so much you

161

couldn't get me in the house fast enough. How you took me on the kitchen counter. Actually, I told him his hand was in the exact spot."

"Wow. You, my love, went for the throat. Good for you. It's about time."

"But there's more. What I shouldn't have thrown in his face. As close as I remember, it was something like you make love to me all night. Not once like he did and roll over and go to sleep. And the real hit right between the eyes was if you were using me, thank the stars for it."

Jacks looked at her for a moment, touched his lips to her forehead. He heard the quiet in his own voice. "Do you think I'm only here for fun? When the deployment happens that's it; until you come to Spain for a booty call?"

Almost at a whisper, she replied, "No. I don't think that. It's been such a short time. I don't understand myself what we are."

He lifted her chin. "Baby, I don't know. There was a connection the day we met. I smiled for days after I changed your tire. I wanted to kiss you; I know it sounds crazy, but you crept into my dreams. I've never been happier; I enjoy our time in and out of bed."

"I feel the same way, but it scares me. The day Troy introduced us I wondered what it would be like to have you touch me."

He closed her in his arms and feasted on her neck. When she drew in a deep breath, he said, "Really, exactly what did you think about?"

"Nothing, forget it."

"No, you don't. Tell me, I'll make you tell, you know I can." He ran his hand along the top of her pants, hooked his fingers in front, and pulled her tight against him. He kissed her neck and whispered, "Or would you rather hear what I thought of doing to you?"

"Jacks!"

"Go ahead, act shocked, play the innocent little girl. I like that. I wondered what treasures I'd find if I followed your legs up under your prim and proper military uniform. Take down your hair and run my fingers through the curls. You haunted my dreams. Night after night, it was your face I saw, those unbelievable eyes."

He took her hand, led her into the house, and slipped the shirt over her head. "What have we here?" He asked as he ran his finger across the sheer fabric covering her breasts.

"It was supposed to be a surprise, after the ride."

A devilish look came into his eyes. "Do the bottoms match?"

"Of course," she whispered.

He undid the buttons of her pants and stepped back. "Take them off, please." His words came in between deep breaths.

She watched his chest rise and fall. "In a minute." Jennifer ran her hands under his shirt. "Take off your shirt."

"Anything for you, my sweet," he whispered.

With the shirt on the floor, she buried her face against the hard muscles of his chest.

He held her at arm's length; his eyes brimmed with passion and tenderness.

"Know this. I'm not here to get lucky. I need you, hell, I have to have you."

She nodded. "Being with you is unbelievable, in bed and out, understand?"

He kissed her nose. "Take off your pants, sexy." His eyes smoldered with fire. "Leave the bra and panties. I want to see your skin against the black."

He kicked off his pants and boxers.

"Let me look at you. Your eyes change to the color of a dark, sweet wine when you start to climb."

She spoke his name and couldn't hold back any longer. He threw a quilt on the floor, and laid her down beside him. "Look at me." He slipped aside the fabric of her panties and joined with her; both flew into the weather of the sexual storm.

In the aftermath, they lay on the quilt, trying to catch their breath. "What time does the ride start?" she asked.

"We have a couple of hours yet. I added extra time. It seems whenever we're alone, we can't keep our hands off each other." Jacks took her hand and kissed it.

"Prepare yourself. I bought a new red leather vest; I think you'll like it."

"Lord help me," he said, helping her up.

"You're the one who started all this," Jennifer whispered and kissed his left nipple.

"Yes, I am. Let's take a shower." He pulled her tight against him.

"I just took one."

"Not like I have in mind," he replied, rubbing his erection against her.

"You are insatiable."

"Come here, and I'll show you."

****

Jacks stood at the kitchen island, sipping champagne. "Brandon, how long after you met Kimberly did you know she was the woman for you?"

He set his glass on the island. "That requires a bit of

backstory. When Dorothy died, my world went to shit. Her long battle with cancer defeated me. I felt like the walking dead. Nothing seemed to matter.

"My commander, who was a good friend, insisted I go to counseling. Actually, it was a direct order. I drove to Langley. I didn't want anyone to know I was seeing a shrink. Jennifer was on call. The first few visits, she let me whine and complain. Wallow in my misery."

"Sounds like what you needed. A shoulder to lean on," Jacks interjected when Brandon took a sip from his glass.

"That's what I thought. Until one visit, she looked me square in the eyes and said, 'Brandon, you know I'm about over your negative bullshit. Put on your big boy boxers and deal with life.' It was like she knew it was time to give me a mental slap."

Jacks leaned against the counter and fought back a smile. A thought that scared him jumped into his mind. *That's my girl.*

"We put together a plan for me to get out a little more each week. Have dinner with friends. Go to the movies. Visit the kids. I began to slip from my depressed muck. Each day the pain was a bit easier to bear.

"I'll admit I had a wild fantasy about Jennifer." Brandon held up his hands as Jacks stiffened in response. "That's all it ever was, fantasy. She was married and made that point very clear."

Jacks relaxed his clenched fists.

"Jennifer says it was fate, but I swear she set Kimberly and me up. They were having dinner at the officer's club. She knew I always ate there before my weekly poker game. Anyway, Jennifer insisted I join them. Kimberly smiled and shook my hand.

"I never made the poker game. It was magical and peaceful at the same time. I'm not sure we knew when Jennifer left. I drove Kimberly home. At the front door, she asked if I was going to kiss her. I did, and it was like being hit with a two-by-four. Two weeks later, I took her away to my cabin in the mountains. We were married after six months."

"Wow. It hit you like that?" Jacks tried to contain his relief. It *was* possible to fall in love this fast.

"Yep, I thought I only needed to get laid. But I never saw love run me over," he added, removing two chilled glasses from the freezer. "Understand, I still miss my Dorothy. But I know she'd be happy for me. Son, has the two-by-four taken you down?"

Jacks looked at the floor, shuffled his feet, and decided to change the subject. If he said the words out loud, it would make them real. "Thanks for suggesting Jennifer and I ride in the limo with you and Kimberly to the party."

Brandon chuckled and poured two more glasses of the bubbly liquid and topped off his own. "No problem. I hoped with Jennifer here Kimberly would be ready on time."

Jacks couldn't suppress his chuckle. "Really? With all due respect, sir, there's a major flaw in your logic."

"In retrospect, it seems very clear. But after seeing the dresses earlier, I'm sure our patience will be rewarded."

"Here, here." Jacks touched his glass to Brandon's. "Our dates are extraordinarily beautiful and intelligent women."

"I'll drink to that toast."

"Toast to what?" Kimberly asked.

Jacks took in the sight of the women standing before him. Jennifer wore a red floor-length dress with a deep V neckline and a front split. Red silk fabric pooled at the matching very high heels. The crisscrossed design at her waist held her ample breasts in place. She turned and showed off the lace cutwork back.

"Since you haven't said a word, I gather you like the dress?" Her voice drew him in.

"Oh yeah, gorgeous, red's your color." He walked to her. "You look sexy as hell," he whispered.

"Thanks. You look pretty good in your dress uniform," Jennifer said, accepting the glass of champagne.

Jacks fought the feelings. He couldn't be in love. It was all hormones. He was enjoying a wonderful sexual relationship. He'd felt this way with his ex. It was just sex. That's all there was then and all it was now. With his feeling explained, he continued to enjoy the evening and the pride he felt with Jennifer on his arm.

Chapter Sixteen

Jennifer watched the clock and tried to concentrate on her client's comments. Instead, all she could think about was the porcelain jewelry box she'd found on her desk. The gifts kept coming—lilies, fruit, a china tea set with painted lilies, and now jewelry. "Do you think he's going to change?" she asked her client.

"I love him. What would I do without him? Who would take care of me?" Darla asked.

"You could take care of yourself." Jennifer hoped the client missed the eye roll and the sarcasm.

"What could I do? Work at McDonalds? I'd never be able to afford my car, much less a place to live." This time her voice was filled with utter panic.

Jennifer took a deep breath and chose her words, perhaps not carefully enough. "Darla, we've been through all this before. You could go to school, join the military. You don't have to have a man to be happy or take care of you. Make yourself happy."

"You can't understand what it's like. You have everything," Darla said and began to cry.

On autopilot, she handed her client a box of tissues. This time Jennifer didn't temper her words. "Darla, we've been working together for eight months. We seem to end up in the same place every session. My life has nothing to do with yours.

"You need to make decisions about your life. If you

want to remain with a man who takes pleasure in beating you, stay. If not, do something about it. Make a plan and follow it." After a brief pause, she continued, "I'm sorry. I don't think you're making the progress you should. I'll refer you to one of my colleagues, someone who could better serve you."

"But I thought we were, like, you know, connecting."

"One of the schedulers will call you next week." Jennifer stood, opened the door, waited for her client to leave, and promptly shut the door. At least she managed not to slam it, even though it would have been an excellent exclamation point.

She opened her desk drawer and removed the cream-colored china box. It was elegantly decorated. Someone had taken great care in hand-painting multiple-colored azaleas with deep emerald green leaves. She opened the box and stared at the pear-cut emerald and white gold earrings and matching necklace. All three stones were at least two carats each. Jacks wouldn't ever give her anything this large and gaudy. He knew her taste. So did Phillip. Who was sending her gifts and why?

A gentle knock shoved her already fragile nerves into overdrive. Her mind raced. It seemed like hours passed before she found her voice to utter two words, "Come in."

Jacks opened the door and stepped into the office. "Hey, sexy, ready for lunch?"

She fought to catch her breath. "Did you send me these?" she asked and held up one of the earrings. Anger shone in his eyes.

"No, I didn't," he said as he stormed to the desk. Took the earring from her and examined it. "You're sure

169

Phillip isn't behind this?"

"This isn't something I wear. He'd know that." She battled to keep the tears in check.

"Then who else?" His voice was smooth but insistent.

"I've been racking my brain trying to figure that out."

Jacks squatted, took her hands, and said, "Baby, you need to call the police."

"I'm going to talk to Phillip. Let him know if anything else happens, I will."

She didn't miss Jacks' sigh of frustration. Or how he shook his head and swallowed the words he wanted to say. "Okay. You ready for lunch?"

"Yes," she responded. But her mind was going ninety miles an hour. She didn't want to talk to Phillip or make Jacks angry. But the answer would come. She couldn't fathom how, but it would.

****

Jennifer pulled into the space in front of the Officer's Club. Phillip was waiting for her at the fountain. She took a deep breath and squared her shoulders as she walked.

"You look tired," Phillip said.

"Let's sit over here." She motioned toward a bench.

He placed his hand in the small of her back as they walked. "What's going on?"

Once they were seated, she began. "I need you to answer a question. Please be honest. It's important."

"Okay."

Her hands were folded in her lap when she spoke. "Have you been sending me gifts?"

His answer was almost instantaneous. "No. Why?"

She watched his eyes. He'd been able to lie to her for so long, she wasn't sure what she expected to see.

"Jennifer, what's wrong?" Now she read concern.

"I've received flowers, fruit, a porcelain tea set, and jewelry. No cards, nothing."

He moved closer and tried to take her hand, but she pulled away. "Where did you find them?"

"The flowers were on my porch at home. The others appeared on my desk."

"Have you contacted the police?"

"No. But if one more thing arrives, I will."

His next questions caught Jennifer off guard. "What does Jacks think?"

"I should call the police now, not wait."

"For once, I agree with him. What about clients? Maybe it's one of the guys from the PTSD group? Perhaps thank you gifts. They're too embarrassed to give them to you in person. I told you this might happen because you connect too closely with your clients."

Jennifer let Phillip's I-told-you-so pass. "I hadn't thought about that. Thanks."

"Is there anything I can do? Put in a security system? I can have the company we use contact you."

"I'll think about it. We have a system. I don't want to scare the girls."

"I understand, but you need to be safe. Please consider an upgrade."

Phillip walked her to the car and took her hand. He turned to face her and put his hands on her shoulders. "Jennifer, I know we've had some bad times, but I'd never do anything to hurt or upset you. Please consider a security system before Jacks deploys." He opened her car door.

Jennifer climbed into the car and buckled her seat belt. It couldn't be Phillip. A client, that possibility never even crossed her mind. Who could it be? Her thoughts froze on one name, Troy. She shook her head. "No way Troy would do this. Would he?"

Chapter Seventeen

Jennifer stopped on the walkway to the three-story painted lady with turrets. Jacks carried their suitcases onto the porch. The ornate Madison home was magnificent with its five-color blends. Blue gingerbread accents made the house pop. The seaside retreat's porch ran the full length of the front of the house. The open section was organized into wicker and wooden sitting areas. A blue, green, and yellow swing hung at the far end of the porch. Jennifer couldn't wait to explore the house. There were multi-colored decorative pitched gables, including one greeting visitors over the front stoop.

The windows were of various sizes and shapes on different floors of the house. Large panes of glass surrounded by small ones filled in the huge windows. Bay, stained glass, and round-arched windows with their asymmetrical designs gave the house a whimsical look. The steepled roof was covered with both slate shingles and patterned wood.

"Baby, are you coming?" Jacks asked from the porch.

"Sure. I was taking in the beautiful house," Jennifer said, and scampered up the six blue, green, and pink stairs.

Max opened the stained-glass front door, walked past his brother, and closed Jennifer in his arms. He kissed her on the cheek and said, "Good to see you. You ready to dump my much older brother and run away with me?"

"Hey, get your hands off my girl," Jacks said, taking Jennifer's hand. He led her into the foyer.

She was greeted by an antique gas chandelier. Hardwood floors spread into an adjacent room with a blue and green tiled fireplace. A fire burned bright behind an ornate black screen. A zigzagged staircase led the way to the second story. A bank of floor-to-ceiling stained glass windows allowed natural lighting behind the stairs and a view of the ocean.

The bright blues, greens, yellows, and pinks were carried throughout the house, which was decorated with eclectic furniture and knickknacks. There were many different eras and colors represented in the living room, but it worked. She at once felt at home.

Jacks placed the suitcases on the first stair and led Jennifer into the kitchen.

"You remember Max, the black sheep of the family, the man who accosted you on the porch."

"My brother's jealous he can't grow a beard like this." Max rubbed his hand across his left cheek

"Or a ponytail," Henry said as he entered the kitchen.

Jennifer watched the two men embrace. There was love there. Henry held Jacks at arm's length. "Good to see you, son."

"It's good to be here, Dad. This is Jennifer Ryan."

Henry Williams embraced Jennifer. "Welcome to our home."

"Hello, beautiful." Alex leaned in and kissed Jennifer on the cheek. "Hey, we have a sister," he added and pulled his brother's ponytail.

Max shot his brother the bird and said, "Fuck you—"

"Maxwell." At the sound of a woman's voice, all four men froze.

"Damn, at least I came prepared," Max said, walking into the kitchen. He pulled a wad of money from his well-worn jeans pocket. He removed two dollar bills and dropped them in the gallon glass jar already half full of bills. "What the hell," he said, dropping all the ones in the jar. "I'll owe you all of it before the weekend is over."

Martha was everything Jennifer remembered from the book signing, all grace and elegance. Her smile was warm and inviting. She hugged Jennifer and stepped back.

"Martha Williams, it's a pleasure to finally meet you."

Her handshake was warm and firm. "Jennifer, please excuse my men's manners. I'm sorry they all have the mouth of a drunken sailor, at least when they arrive."

Martha laughed and pointed to the jar, "Every time they use a curse word, it costs them a dollar in the jar. It's my fun money. This weekend, it's our spa fund."

"No problem. Being military, I've heard that word and many others. We've met before. My daughters and I had lunch with you in Atlanta about eight years ago. They still have the autographed pictures hanging in their room."

"I love those events. I can't wait to get reacquainted with you and your daughters. I have a new series coming out in January."

"Oh, I know. My girls follow you on social media. When the announcement came out about the new series they called me at work to share the news. I haven't told them you're Jacks' mother. I wanted to talk with you first."

"It's fine. As for the social media, I have someone, somewhere, who oversees all that. It's Greek to me." Martha waved her hands in the air. "Would you like a cup of tea?"

"That would be wonderful."

"Gentlemen, any of you want to join us for tea?" Martha asked as she poured water into a white teapot decorated with multicolored dancing dachshunds. Jennifer recognized it from the prints in Martha's books.

The responses from the four men were various. All meant no to her offer. "Beer's in the refrigerator in the butler's pantry." With that, the men were gone. "I made white ginger tea. Hope that's okay?"

"Sure. You have a lovely kitchen. It looks vintage. You have the upgrades cleverly camouflaged."

"With Henry in the Navy, we moved every two to three years. When we bought this house and did the remodel, I wanted the kitchen to keep its charm. At the same time, I wanted all the fancy appliances and latest gadgets. Henry made it happen."

Martha added a dachshund-shaped cream pitcher, cut glass bowls of lemon wedges, and sugar cubes to the table.

"Let's sit over here by the bay window. We can chat and watch the waves," Martha said and carried the tray to the round iron and wood table.

Jennifer selected a high-back chair with a bright, colorful cushion. "The view is breathtaking," she said, looking out the windows at the surf.

"Yes, it's so peaceful. I love to escape here."

"Do you visit here often?" Jennifer asked as Martha arranged the china on the table.

"Several times a year." Martha leaned in before she continued. "Between you and me, I'd love to sell the house in Cambridge and live here full time, but Henry would be lost without his host of friends. He's more of a social butterfly than I am." She smiled and poured tea into the cups. "But I'll wear him down with time."

"Here come the hounds," a voice announced from somewhere outside the kitchen.

"You have dachshunds?" Jennifer heard the excitement in her own voice as she dropped two small sugar cubes into her cup.

"Always, you'll have to tell them *down* unless you want to play."

Jennifer smiled as the three dachshunds rounded the corner into the kitchen and headed straight to the table at full gallop. One was a long hair black and tan, another with a smooth red coat, and the third a chocolate dapple wirehair. "They're so cute."

"Sit," Martha said. All three stopped jumping and placed their rumps on the floor. They wiggled in place.

She reached into a ceramic container and pulled out three small dog biscuits. Martha pointed to the black and tan dog and handed him a treat, "This is Houdini, so named because he is an escape artist. Scarlet, well, it's simple. Her coat is such a lovely shade of red." Martha handed Scarlet a biscuit. "Finally, the clown of the bunch, Skipper." She handed the wirehair a treat. "I wanted to call him Admiral, but that was voted down by Henry."

Jennifer leaned in and petted each of the dogs. Skipper took off into the living room and returned with a ball in his mouth. He sat up on his haunches. "He looks like he's smiling."

"Yes. I love the face. Let me warn you, before you take the ball, once you throw it, he'll never leave you alone."

Jennifer took the ball and rolled it across the kitchen. Skipper was back in seconds staring at Jennifer. "You are too cute," Jennifer said, rolling the ball again.

****

Jacks strolled into the kitchen. He smiled at the sight of his mother and Jennifer, shoulder to shoulder, laughing at a photo album.

"Hey there, you certainly were a cute kid," Jennifer said.

Jacks watched the grin grow on her face.

"Really, Mom, you could've waited a few days to pull out the pictures."

"I think Jennifer can manage seeing you in diapers," she said with a chuckle.

Jacks walked behind the ladies and placed a hand on each shoulder. A rush of emotions flowed through him. Was this love? A warm, peaceful contentment.

Jacks' thought process was interrupted by Jennifer's snicker.

She smiled up at Jacks. "You're such a cutie, the sheriff rounding up the outlaws." Jennifer pointed to a picture of all the boys. Jacks was wearing chaps, six-shooters, and a cowboy hat. Alex and Max were wearing bandannas covering the nose and mouth, both with their hands in the air. Jacks had his gun pointed at the pair.

"He always kept his brothers in line. I think several pieces of my good silver disappeared, or maybe it was the pirates' hidden-treasure phase," Martha said, placing her hand on Jacks'. "I miss those days."

"Kids grow up too fast. One day, they're underfoot making you crazy, and the next, they have their own lives," Jennifer said.

"Before I go too far down memory lane and have a cry, let's start dinner. Jacks, will you get the charcoal started?"

"Sure." Jacks was enjoying the warm interaction between Jennifer and his mom. He decided to kill two birds with one stone. Tease his mom and conduct the task she'd given him. He stepped into the hall and yelled, "Max, Mom says start the charcoal."

When he turned around, his mother stood, hands on her hips. "I could have done that."

Jacks stepped to her, kissed her cheek, and wrapped her in his arms. "I love you, Mommy," he whispered.

Martha laughed and pushed him gently back. "Now you're kissing up."

Jacks looked at the ceiling and whistled. "Wow, tough crowd. Why don't I pour wine if you two are done with tea?"

"Great idea," Jennifer said.

"I agree," Martha said and began removing things from the refrigerator. She turned to Jennifer and said, "I hope you like salmon and lobster?"

"I certainly do. What can I do to help?"

"Mom, Jennifer makes the most incredible lobster stew and homemade bread."

"I'll need your lobster stew recipe," Martha said as she placed a large red bowl filled to the top with vegetables on the counter. "Do you mind making a salad?"

"Not at all," Jennifer said.

"The cutting boards are in the cupboard in front of you, and knives are in the drawer to the left."

Jacks leaned against the counter, opened the bottle of white wine, and watched the two women. Jennifer seemed to be fitting in well with his family. Something his ex-wife never seemed to be able to do after years of marriage.

Chapter Eighteen

Jennifer snuggled under the covers. She should get up and do something, anything, but the bed felt wonderful. She'd read the paper and completed the crossword puzzle. Maybe she'd work in the yard. Ten more minutes and she'd get up and get moving. Her cell broke her concentration. She looked at the caller ID. It was Lisa.

"Hey, Lisa, everything okay?" she asked.

"I'm okay." There was something in her tone, but Jennifer couldn't get a fix on it. "The girls weren't feeling well last night. They want to come home if it's okay."

Jennifer shifted up in the bed. "Sure. What's the matter?"

"Morgan says cramps, but it seems like more than that. I didn't want to push."

"Do you want me to pick them up?"

"No. I'll bring them. About an hour, okay?"

"That's fine. Lisa, are you okay?" Jennifer climbed from the bed and slipped on her sandals.

"I'm tired and worried about the girls."

"Thanks for taking good care of them. They love you very much. I don't worry when they're with you. See you soon."

Jennifer collected the newspaper spread all over the bed, placed it on the cedar chest, and made the bed. She headed downstairs to make a cup of coffee. The sound in Lisa's voice still troubled her. She was finishing up an email when the girls arrived.

"Hello there. I understand you aren't feeling well?" Jennifer said as she hugged her daughters. Touched them on the forehead to check for a temp. But she knew from the look on their faces something was very wrong.

Morgan took Lisa's hand. "Mom, can Miss Lisa stay for breakfast?"

"Yes. Can you please stay?" Madison asked.

"No. I better go. Phillip's waiting," Lisa said.

The same stressed tone still rang in Lisa's voice. Her eyes were ringed in dark circles, and Jennifer caught fear in her eyes. "Girls take your things to your room, Lisa, can you stay and have a cup of coffee?"

"I better not. I need to get back," Lisa clutched her purse to her chest.

"You sure you're okay?" Jennifer asked and stepped closer to her.

"Yes. Not myself, I guess." She shrugged her shoulders.

Jennifer placed her hand on Lisa's shoulder. "You know you can talk to me, right? We got off to a shaky start, but I don't blame you for anything. Is Phillip hurting you?"

"I'm fine, really." She placed her hand on Jennifer's.

Jennifer locked eyes with Lisa. "If he's mistreating you, I'm here for you. Just tell me what's going on. I of all people know now he can be."

"Like I said, I'll be okay."

She didn't believe her but let it go. As Lisa opened the door, Jennifer said, "Lisa, you know I'm here for you; just reach out."

Lisa hesitated. Jennifer thought she was going to say something important. Instead, her response was, "Thank you. That means more than you can know."

As Lisa backed from the driveway, she knew something was wrong. Jennifer had read fear, stark and vivid in Lisa's hollow eyes. Yes, something was very wrong.

She took the stairs two at a time and rushed down the hall to the twins' room, "Okay, spill it. What happened? Why is Lisa so upset?" she asked the two girls sitting on the ends of their beds.

The unwelcomed tension stretched even tighter when neither spoke. She looked back and forth from Madison to Morgan. Tears were their only response. The silence hung between them like a mist.

Jennifer opened her arms wide. The twins stepped to her, and she folded them in her arms. "Whatever it is, we'll get through it," Jennifer whispered and kissed each girl on the forehead.

"Mom, it's awful. Daddy hit Lisa and said terrible things about us," Madison managed between sobs.

For a long while, a tense silence enveloped the room. Jennifer held the girls and let them cry. "Okay, let's sit down and talk this out." *This had to be a terrible misunderstanding.*

****

"Jennifer moved the coffee cup around the table and watched traffic out the diner window. Rain drops fell in slow motion from the red-striped awnings. The interaction with Lisa and what her daughters shared played over and over in her head. The situation left her stunned and angry.

As Jennifer grabbed her purse to leave Lisa carried

Phillip, Jr. into the small restaurant.

"I'm sorry, I'm late. I had to wait for Phillip to leave for work. He'd kill me if he knew I was talking to you about this." Her words game out in breathless, rapid succession.

"It's okay, What's going on? The girl's told me he hit you." Jennifer watched the tears pool in Lisa's eyes.

"Just start from the beginning. We'll figure it out."

****

Jennifer placed the pot of chili and platter of chocolate cupcakes on the table in the fellowship hall. "Have a good time in Washington. I'll see you Sunday," she said and hugged her daughters. Fought the tears. Where had the years gone? Her toddlers had transformed into beautiful young women.

Driving home, a wave of loneliness rolled over her like dark rain clouds stealing a clear summer day. Feelings of doom blanketed her world. She wondered if Lisa had been able to stand up to Phillip, but she'd done all she could. Unless Lisa told him, Phillip wouldn't have any idea she was part of the plan. Poor thing, Phillip had put Lisa through hell. But that wasn't her problem. Jennifer had to deal with the fallout of Madison and Morgan hearing their father's comments. *Don't think about it now!*

Tomorrow, with the girls out of town, she'd address the situation with Phillip, which would be soon enough. Like other problems, they'd sit down and work through it. He'd be angry and blame everyone else, but for his girls, he'd do anything. No problem was too big to solve, her inner psychologist reassured her, and she dismissed the situation. Think positive.

Jacks, the thought of him made her smile. She had a

care package to fill with cookies and goodies. How she missed him, he'd been gone for three months. In two weeks, she'd meet him in Spain. She'd concentrate on that.

As the garage door slammed shut, Jennifer spoke to herself in the rearview mirror. "Okay, silly woman, get your butt out of the car. Go work on the girls' quilts, put together the care package, and stay busy."

She walked into the house and poured a glass of wine. After changing into her new dachshund pajamas, she headed to the sewing room. The doorbell stopped her.

She opened the door to Phillip. Dread hit. She wasn't ready for this conversation. "The girls aren't here; they're headed to DC with the church youth group."

"I know where the fuck my daughters are. I came to talk to you," he barked and stepped in the doorway.

The strong odor of booze hit her before the words. She let out a long slow breath. This was all she needed. "Okay." Jennifer ran her fingers through her hair and placed her hands on her hips.

"First, you have that dumb-ass naval aviator around my girls. Now you're telling them lies, and they hate me."

"Phillip, we've had this conversation before, my life with Jacks is none of your business, and I've told the girls nothing. You need to leave; you're drunk. We'll talk tomorrow as planned." She retreated to close the door.

He shoved the door toward her, and the force threw Jennifer against the wall. The impact caused a moment of disorientation. She shook her head to clear the fog. "Phillip, what are you thinking?" The metallic taste of fear and panic hit the back of her throat.

"You, stupid, arrogant bitch! Did you think I'd roll over and let you ruin my life?" Phillip raged and slammed the door.

Jennifer knew she had to calm the situation.

****

Jacks checked his watch and finished the third lap around the hangar deck. One more lap he'd shower and video chat with Jennifer. The warmth in his stomach made him smile. Two weeks and they'd be together in Rota. He'd propose. They'd make love in the moonlight.

The mental picture caused him to quicken his pace. Jacks was deep into a daydream about his last night with Jennifer when the Air Boss shouted his name.

"Sir?" Jacks asked as he ran in place facing the captain.

"Skipper wants to see you."

"Yes, sir. I'll shower and head up."

The senior officer looked over his glasses and stated, "Old Man said now."

"Yes, sir, like I said, on my way," Jacks replied and began to double-time it up the multiple ladders to the superstructure of the Bird Farm.

He knocked on the outer door to Brandon's office.

"Enter," Brandon bellowed.

"You wanted to see me, sir?" Jacks asked entering the office. Jennifer's comment that he was a big teddy bear popped into his head.

Brandon walked around his desk, sat on the edge, and pointed to the chair. "Yes. Take a seat."

"Yes, sir," Jacks did as he was told as his stomach churned. Something bad was going on. He hardly, if ever, saw Brandon while they were deployed. It was an unwritten understanding between the two. Their relationship was different on the boat.

Brandon leaned in as he spoke. "Son, there's no way to sugarcoat this. Jennifer was attacked sometime yesterday. As of thirteen hundred local, she was in surgery. Kimberly promised to keep us updated."

"Is it bad? Is she going to be okay? Do they know who attacked her?" Jacks asked in rapid succession as he stood and paced around the room. Panic began to overtake him.

Brandon picked up a piece of paper from his desk. "Kimberly said they took a Mr. Macintyre into custody—"

Jacks turned quickly and stood statue still. "No way in hell Troy would hurt Jennifer!" Jacks yelled. His mind spun—wait. Troy had a truck, he had access to the clinic to leave gifts, and he'd talked about Jennifer when he'd been drunk. Many things fell into place. Could Troy have been the stalker? Jacks shook his head.

Brandon put his hand on Jacks' shoulder. "Troy was agitated and covered in blood when police and emergency services arrived. They took him into custody."

"What else did Kimberly say about Jennifer's condition?" Jacks asked, rubbing the back of his neck.

"From the initial exam, it's bad. It's touch and go at this point."

Jacks stopped and turned to Brandon. "Oh, shit, what about Morgan and Madison?"

"They were on a church trip in Washington, DC. Lisa and her dad flew to pick them up. Until the situation is sorted out, Wallingford's security chief has around the clock guards with Jennifer and the girls."

"That's good." The thought gave Jacks momentary relief as he caught his quickening breath. "Any idea when we might get an update?"

"I'm not sure. But I have an idea," Brandon said, returning to his desk.

"What?" Jacks asked, trying to focus and calm the alarm bells clanging in his mind.

"There's a medevac plane arriving in about three hours for patient transport. I have appointed you Officer in Charge to supervise the transfer in Norfolk."

"But we're already down two pilots," Jacks blurted but grasped on the thought of getting to Jennifer.

"Let me worry about that," Brandon said with a wave of his hand. "My yeoman's cutting your orders as we speak."

"Thanks," Jacks said, returning to the chair. "I'll email my parents. I can use their support. Plus, Dad can run interference if there's issues with Jennifer's care."

"Use my phone. Tell them you'll be there Tuesday," Brandon stood, removed a cigar from his desk, and headed for the door.

"Thank you, sir," Jacks said, jumping to attention as Brandon passed.

"I'll keep you all in my prayers," the captain said as he paused briefly beside Jacks.

Jacks' hands shook as he dialed his parents' number and told them what had happened. They assured him they'd head for Virginia immediately. Jacks went to his rack and lay in the dark thinking about Jennifer. He'd known he loved her, hell, for a while, yet continued to fight the feelings. Common sense told him no one falls in love so fast. But his heart said something else. If Jennifer died, he'd never be able to tell her.

His thoughts raced. His stomach churned. Jennifer and the girls sent letters, emails, and baked cookies for his command. The packages, letters, and emails arrived like clockwork. The guys in the shop teased him about the pictures he was always sharing; but no one turned down the goodies.

The love for all three of them only drove his panic. How were his girls? Madison and Morgan were his girls, just as if he'd given them life, and he needed to get to them. They'd be scared and confused. He should have called them. Or better yet called Phillip. Surely given the circumstances he'd put aside his petty jealousy.

But how could he help them? What could he say or do? Could Troy have attacked Jennifer? The shock had begun to wear off and was quickly replaced by rage. He'd hunt the son of a bitch down, make him pay. Troy would simply disappear; they'd never find the body.

Jacks climbed from his rack and headed topside. He needed to clear his mind if that was even possible. He stood on the deck and let the emotions come. For the first time in years, he cried. The strong, salty breeze forced the tears into his skin.

He felt so lost, so helpless, so out of control. He looked out over the dark sea and prayed his thoughts would somehow reach Jennifer. Let her know he was on the way. Everything would be okay. A wave of nausea hit with full force. Could it ever be the same? Yes, he'd make it okay, no matter what it took.

****

Jacks wanted to shove the young pilot from the seat and take control of the plane. Could the guy possibly taxi any slower? On the tarmac, Jacks handed the patient and paperwork to the corpsman and sprinted to the command hangar at Norfolk Air Station.

His parents waited inside the terminal. "Hello, son," Henry said as the two embraced.

"Dad. Thanks for being here," Jacks replied and turned to his mother.

"Mom." He hugged her and held on tight. She provided the temporary comfort he needed. Jacks struggled to control his tears. "Have you seen Jennifer?"

"Yes, last night and this morning," Henry said taking Jacks' bag.

"How is she?" Jacks asked in a hopeful whisper.

Martha took her son's hand. "Alex says Jennifer will be fine. She'll need time and lots of support, the road to a full recovery will be a long one."

"Alex?" Jacks asked, surprise lacing his question.

"I called him, he headed to the hospital. Watched the surgery and spoke with Jennifer's care team, stayed with her until we arrived."

Jacks let out a deep breath, the first one since he'd spoken with Brandon. If Alex said Jennifer would be fine, he was sure she would. Man, he loved his family.

"What about the twins?" He heard his voice crack.

"Lisa says they're doing as well as could be expected. We had dinner with them last night. They keep asking when you'll be here."

"Where are they?" Jacks asked.

Henry answered this time. "At the Wallingfords' with Lisa. Adam insisted we park our motor coach there. There are guards with Jennifer around the clock. Max is there also."

"What the hell is he doing here?" Jacks shouted over his mother's shoulder at Troy.

Henry placed his hand on Jacks shoulder. "Son,

Phillip was the attacker, not Troy. If he hadn't been there to call for help, Jennifer would have died. He's wanted to talk to you," Henry said.

Jacks walked to Troy. His shoulders were hunched, his face was full of dread, and his eyes were bloodshot.

"I'm sorry," Troy said.

Jacks embraced his friend. "Dad says Jennifer would've died if you hadn't been there," he whispered in his friend's ear.

Troy stepped back and said, "I watched over her like I said. I should have checked on her earlier—"

"No. Listen, you did everything right. I owe you. We'll talk later," Jacks said.

"Has Phillip been arrested?" Jacks asked the group.

Troy seemed to have his bearings again and answered, "Not yet. The police verified via a bloody fingerprint he was the attacker. Jennifer scratched him. There was DNA under her fingernails. It's been sent out for testing."

"Let's go. I want to see Jennifer and then the girls," Jacks said. The relief his parents provided gave way as the sense of urgency returned. He'd have to be strong for them no matter what happened. They were his family now. He'd deal with Phillip later.

****

Jacks' mind raced, his thoughts running amuck as they entered the hospital. Pain, hate, and fear seemed to pelt his body from all directions.

Kimberly met him outside the ICU.She folded him in her arms and held him tight.

He took a deep breath and stepped back. "I understand the overall news is good."

Kimberly took a deep breath and turned. "Henry,

191

Martha, Troy, Mr. Wallingford had lunch delivered. It's set up in conference room three fifty-six." She motioned to her left down the hall.

"Thank you. Son, let us know when you're ready to see the girls," Henry said and patted his son's shoulder.

Kimberly turned to Jacks. "Let's sit over here. Jennifer woke about an hour ago and asked for you. I told her you were on your way. We need to talk before you go in. She looks bad. Phillip did a real number on her. There are multiple broken bones and internal damage. Small cuts all over her body. There's damage consistent with a violent rape. The jerk cut her hair at the base of her skull."

Jacks stared at the floor as an invisible fist punched him in the chest, and he fought to breathe. His fists clenched at his sides; he wanted to hit something.

Kimberly took his hand and whispered, "Jacks, we need to talk."

"Okay." The air around his body seemed to pulse as he waited for Kimberly to continue. He shifted his eyes to hers.

She played with the small pearl earring in her left ear. "I don't mean to be blunt, but I feel I have to. The girls asked when you were coming. They're really counting on you. If you're not one hundred percent in, you need to walk away now, for everyone's sake."

Jacks reached into his pocket and removed a box. "I was going to ask Jennifer to marry me in Spain." He played with the crimson box and faced Kimberly again. "I knew I loved her before I deployed. I couldn't make myself say the words."

Kimberly patted his hand. "She's going to be okay. It'll take time. She's getting the best care possible.

Everyone at the hospital loves her. Not to mention your father is good friends with the hospital commander." She smiled and rubbed her hands together. "Well, are you going to let me see the ring?"

Jacks opened the box. "Do you think she'll like it?"

"Wow. Are you kidding?" She fixed her gaze on the ring. "Let me see if I know jewelry. Two carat, emerald-cut diamond, in a platinum setting."

"Yep. My plan was to video chat with the girls while Jennifer was traveling to Spain. Make sure they were okay with my proposing to their mom."

"They'll be thrilled. Please don't take offense by my questions. I had to be sure about your intentions."

"None taken. You're a good friend. Jennifer's lucky to have you," Jacks said, returning the ring to his jacket pocket.

Kimberly stood and said, "Come on. Let me introduce you to the guards. Max went for coffee a couple of minutes ago."

Jacks entered intensive care and was glad his sweetheart was asleep. It took him a minute to mask his shock. He expelled an exasperated sigh. Anger surged through his body.

Jennifer's face was swollen and bruised. If Kimberly hadn't led him to the room, he wouldn't have known it was Jennifer. There were tubes, wires, and machines churning away. He walked to the bedside, placed his hand against hers, and whispered, "Sweetheart, I'm here."

He watched her attempt to open her eyes. The left one was swollen shut. "Jacks, I'm so sorry," her voice was garbled, harsh, and raspy.

He closed his hand around hers. "What do you have

to be sorry for?"

"I should've listened," she explained.

"Baby, that doesn't matter. I wish I'd been wrong." He wanted to touch her but wasn't sure where he could without hurting her.

"Are the girls okay?" she asked between deep breaths, struggling to speak each word.

"They're safe. Adam has guards at the house. I'm going to see them later."

"How long can you stay?" Jennifer asked as a tear rolled down her right cheek.

"Two weeks or so," Jacks forced a smile. How could he ever leave her like this? His dad could pull strings and keep him here. He'd never asked for a favor before. Maybe it was time.

He sat on the bedside and held her hand. Her breathing steadied as she drifted off to sleep.

Max entered the room carrying two cups of coffee. He set the tray on the table. "You look like shit," he said to Jacks before pulling him into a bear hug.

Jacks stepped back and pulled his brother's ponytail. "Good to see you, too."

"Got here as quick as I could. Alex went home to shower. You know, pretty boy's shirt was wrinkled." Max paused, leaned in, and whispered, "You should've seen our baby brother being all professional. It was downright scary."

Jacks decided not to point out that time-wise Max was born last, which made him the actual baby of the family, but decided to let that continual joke go. Plus, the friendly banter was helping the ache assaulting his body. "Couldn't have been as bad as watching you work the room at one of your high-dollar meet-the-author book signings."

Max let his shoulders rise and fall before pulling Jacks into the corner. "So, we gonna kick that son of a bitch Phillip's ass?"

"First thing on my list after things here straighten out. I knew something was off, but I had no idea he was this dangerous." Jacks picked up one of the coffees and took a large gulp.

"Just say the word, brother. I still have contacts from when I wrote *Warrior's Advance.* A couple of those wise guys owe me."

Jacks was about to respond when Jennifer called his name. Jacks said, "I'm right here, baby."

"I'll be outside," Max said.

"You are here. It wasn't a dream," Jennifer said.

"Nope, I'm right here," Jacks said, stroking her hand. I need a favor," her voice was raspy and raw.

"Anything, baby."

"I don't want the girls to see me like this. It's hard enough for them to understand." Each sentence was punctuated by her struggling to take a breath. The machines chimed and beeped. "Phillip was drunk. He said and did terrible things. He cut my hair," she said as the tears pooled in her eyes, and she stroked the short curls.

Jacks stood and leaned in. "Sweetheart, I know. None of this is your fault. We'll work though it together. Besides, I like short hair." He swallowed hard, trying to subdue the outrage.

Her voice was ragged now. "I'm glad you're here. I missed you so much. Can you hold me, please?"

He carefully moved the wires and tubes, gathered her in his arms, and held her tight while she sobbed. He whispered, "Sweetheart, we'll get through this. I promise. I love you." Jacks stroked her hair.

"Oh, Jacks, I love you, too."

His heart soared. Feelings he never knew existed filled his body. This was what so many of his friends talked about. The words *I love you* danced in his brain.

Jennifer continued, "I wanted to tell you before you deployed. I was scared."

Jacks could tell each word was a struggle. He spoke softly, "I understand. I was afraid, too. I knew I loved you from the day I carried you into the emergency room. Remember what I said?"

Jennifer tried to smile but winced in pain. "Yes."

"You rest. I'll go and talk to Madison and Morgan. Will you try to sleep while I go? I'm not sure what to say."

"You'll figure it out. I know you will."

His anger abated somewhat under the warmth of her forced smile. He'd kill Phillip if he could find him. But the clamp of pain around his heart released some. They'd be okay. He'd make it okay. Jacks wasn't sure how, but he'd find a way through this fog.

****

Jennifer clung to Jacks. "Will you come back?"

He placed his forehead gently on hers. "Just try and stop me. As soon as I'm sure the girls are okay, I'll be back." He took her hand again. "Kimberly and Max are outside; they'll be with you until I get back. Don't worry, you're safe. Adam arranged guards twenty-four seven."

"Okay. Jacks?"

"Yes?"

"Will you say it again?"

His grin made her smile inside. "What? Oh, that.

Jennifer, I love you."

"I love you, too."

Jacks left the room, and thoughts flooded Jennifer's mind. *You say you love me. But did you really feel that way before? Or are you saying it to make me feel better? What happens if I can't make love to you after this? Our sex life was amazing. We connected on so many levels. Phillip was right, I'll always think about what he did when we're together.* Tears began to sting the stitches on her face. *I may not be able to have children. Jacks deserves a whole woman. Someone he can be with in every way, give him a son.* She closed her eyes and let the wall of sadness close around her.

Chapter Nineteen

Jacks watched the men at the gate to the Wallingford Estate. He counted three. A fourth approached the vehicle. The driver rolled down the window. Jacks listen to the exchange.

"I have Admiral and Mrs. Williams, and Commander Williams," the driver said. The guard's response was short and to the point. "Charlie is waiting at the house." Then he stepped aside.

The two wrought iron gates slowly opened. The black ornamental scrolls were adorned with metal roses and leaves of various colors. The more-than-a-mile long driveway was lined with colorful shrubs and flowers. Normally it would be a wonderful greeting. But dread and fear hung over Jacks.

The car stopped in front of a large colonial home. Almost at once, the limo door was opened.

"Hello, Admiral and Mrs. Williams," a very large man said as he helped Martha out of the limo.

"Hello, Charlie," they both responded.

Jacks followed his parents from the limo. He was greeted with an extended hand. "Mr. Williams, I'm Charlie McManus, Head of Wallingford security."

Jacks spoke as they shook hands, "I guess I have you to thank for the security at the hospital?"

"Glad to handle it. Dr. Ryan is special to all of us. If you will follow me, Miss Morgan and Miss Madison are in the atrium having lunch."

"How are they doing?" Jacks asked as they walked.

"Confused. But who can blame them? They seemed a bit better when I told them you had arrived. How is Dr. Ryan?"

"As well as can be expected, I guess. We talked for a while. I told her I was coming to see the girls. Is there any progress on locating Phillip?"

Charlie stopped and turned to face Jacks. "No. Part of me hopes the police find him first. The other part would like to have an up close and personal conversation with the son of a bitch. Guess I shouldn't say that."

Jacks placed his hand on Charlie's shoulder and said, "I never liked the guy from day one. I knew he was trouble, but I had no idea he was capable of this. You find him and the three of us will have a talk. Then the police can have him." Jacks' fatigue and frustration poured out.

"We'll find Phillip. You concentrate on Dr. Ryan and the girls."

Jacks followed Charlie into the house, through the library, and into the atrium.

"Mr. Jacks, you're here. How's Mom?" Madison asked as she and Morgan ran toward him. Jacks wrapped them in his arms and held tight. He slowly released the twins and whispered, "Your mom is going to be okay."

Madison turned and headed back to the table. Morgan paused and stared into Jacks' eyes. He watched the tears well up as she spoke. "Is it true what they are saying about Dad? He hurt Mom?"

Jacks led Madison to the table and sat between the two girls. "Yes, sweetie, I'm sorry, it is." He fought the urge to tell the girls what a son of a bitch their father was, but that wasn't what Jennifer would do. She'd take the high road, so he would, too.

He took a deep breath and took both girls' hands. "Your father isn't a bad person. He acted out of anger and emotion. I'm sure he regrets what he did."

Morgan took a few seconds to process the words and asked, "Then why is he hiding? If he knows he did this awful thing, why not turn himself in?

Jacks heart was breaking. "Morgan, I don't know. I wish I could explain."

She returned her attention back to her lunch and asked in a whisper, "You've seen Mom? Is she really going to be, okay?"

"Yes. It's going to take a while, but she'll be okay. We talked; she sends her love."

"Miss Lisa says we can't go see her yet," Madison whispered.

"I think that's best for a while. She needs to rest. We can call her if you like. How does that sound?"

"Okay," Morgan said.

"Good," Madison added, sliding the food around her plate.

Jacks couldn't miss that she was too quiet and not herself. Both girls were, like their mother, almost always laughing and smiling, but not today. Given the situation, that was to be expected.

"I thought your parents were coming," Madison finally said, breaking the silence.

"They'll be right in. Mr. Wallingford asked them to stay in the house. They'll be in the room next to yours."

Jacks turned his attention to Morgan as they left the atrium and headed to the living room. He lightly brushed his arm against Morgan's. "Sweetie, what's wrong?"

"Nothing," she said, shrugging her shoulders.

"You tell him, or I will," Madison said from the doorway.

Jacks sat on an ottoman and motioned toward the love seat. "Girls, please sit. Tell me what's going on."

The girls looked at the floor. Finally, Morgan whispered, "This is my fault."

"What's your fault?" Jacks asked, squeezing her hand,

Their eyes met for a brief second before she spoke. "The reason Daddy hurt Mom."

"Okay. You're going to have to explain. How can any of this be your fault?" Jacks asked, quickly looking from one scared face to another.

"Morgan and I were watching television. We heard Daddy and Miss Lisa fighting again."

Jacks held their hands and asked, "Again? What do you mean again?"

Morgan answered this time. "They fought a lot. I know it was wrong. But we listened from the top of the stairs."

Jacks leaned forward. "Go ahead. We'll talk about the listening in later."

"Daddy blamed Miss Lisa for breaking up our family," Morgan said.

"Which isn't true," Madison quickly added.

Morgan continued staring at the floor. "Miss Lisa said Dad told her he was single when they met. He told her Mom was a mean, hateful person, but Lisa said that was a lie."

The girls continued to take turns telling Jacks the story. "Dad called Miss Lisa an ungrateful bitch and said Mom wasn't really her friend. That we only put up with her because Mom told us too, and we didn't love her either. How could she expect us to after she broke up our family?"

When Morgan began to cry, Madison continued the story. "He called Miss Lisa a fat slut. He hit her. We heard it. He said something about pictures he'd put on the internet. Morgan went to bed. I made a lot of noise like I was coming down the stairs. I told them Morgan was sick; Daddy sent me back upstairs."

"But you didn't, did you?" Jacks asked, trying not to sound too harsh. His feelings toward Phillip were spiraling out of control.

Morgan shook her head, and the tears started again. Madison put her arm around her sister and continued. "Dad told Miss Lisa to go take care of the two idiots. He called us idiots. Told Miss Lisa the only reason he had us come over was to hurt Mom. When Lisa came to our room, there was a handprint on her face."

"That's when we told her we wanted to go home. The next morning, she called Mom."

"Mom said she knew something was wrong the minute she saw us. After Miss Lisa left, she came to our room, and we told her everything."

While he listened, his blood boiled, but he held his emotions in check. "Knowing your mom, she went straight to help Lisa."

Madison finished the story. "If we hadn't told Mom, she wouldn't have gone to see Lisa. Lisa wouldn't have made Daddy leave, and he wouldn't have hurt Mom."

He took their hands again. "Listen, both of you, none of this is your fault. Your father made bad choices. You did the right thing telling your mom. What you did wrong was listening in on an adult conversation. You'll learn as you get older that sometimes it's better not to have all the answers. If you do, you have to deal with the ramifications." *Damn, he sounded like his father.*

"But you did the right thing. Even if things did turn out bad, it will get better. Your mom will be fine."

"Okay," both girls said.

When his words didn't seem to help, he tried another approach. "Look. Have I ever lied to you about anything? Even when the answer was something you didn't want to hear?"

"No, sir." Morgan said.

"Madison?"

"No, sir."

"This isn't your fault. All of this happened because of decisions your dad made. Phillip isn't a bad person." *He was a crazy, raging mad man,* was what he wanted to say, but the girls didn't need to hear that.

"Your dad did something very wrong. It happens all the time, especially when alcohol is involved. Don't beat yourselves up, okay? Now, why don't we call Kimberly and see if your mom's awake." Jacks noticed the girls looked a bit better. He'd done the right thing, spoken the truth. But parenting was way off his radar. Jennifer would have to teach him how it worked. Another truth hit him square between the eyes. When he and Jennifer married, he'd be a father of teenagers. The thought scared him but made him smile at the same time.

****

Jacks was headed back to the hospital when Charlie caught up with him. "Mr. Williams, if you have a minute, Mr. Wallingford would like to speak with you."

"Lead the way. Is there any new information on Phillip?"

"No, not yet. He's either very smart or lucky. I think we know which one it is. Mr. Wallingford's in here," Charlie said, opening the study door.

"Mr. Wallingford," Jacks said, extending his hand.

Jacks checked out the tall, slender man who looked much different than he'd expected. His hair was completely gray, as was his tightly trimmed beard and mustache. Adam Wallingford was thin and trim and stood at least six feet.

"The pleasure is all mine. Morgan and Madison were ecstatic when they heard you were coming home. Please call me Adam. Would you like something to drink? I have a bottle of a smooth sour mash whiskey."

"I could use that about now," Jacks said, running his hand over his chin.

"Over ice work?" Adam asked as he walked toward the bar.

"Wonderful."

"Have a seat," Adam said, pointing to the sitting area as he poured two drinks. He handed Jacks a glass. Adam spoke as he sat adjacent to his guest. "I don't know Jennifer very well; we've spoken at events for the girls. How is she doing?"

Jacks understood polite society conversations. Adam was getting a feel for Jacks before he moved to what was on his mind. This man had eyes and ears everywhere. Jacks decided to go with the flow and sip the smooth bourbon.

"She's doing as well as can be expected. The girls spoke with her earlier."

"Good. Your parents have accepted my invitation to stay on the estate. I hope you will, as well."

"Thank you, I'll be spending most of my time with

Jennifer and the rest with the girls. They're safe here. That's important."

"I'm happy to help. Phillip Ryan is my problem and has been since he met my daughter."

"Any idea what set him off?"

Adam sipped his drink, giving himself time to compose his words. "It began with Morgan and Madison telling their mom about a conversation they overheard. Jennifer asked Lisa to have lunch, and the two discussed the situation.

"My daughter broke down and told Jennifer several things about her marriage." He paused long enough to take a sip of his drink.

"Phillip had been abusing Lisa mentally and sexually. She felt helpless because he had pictures of her in less than flattering situations. She'd been drugged and forced to take part in some activities, shall we say, that would allow Phillip to prove her an unfit mother. Our two ladies decided to take care of things."

Jacks stopped his glass in midair. "Why am I not surprised?"

"Me, either. They asked me to take Phillip to lunch and golfing. Told me they wanted him out of the house for several hours. Some sort of surprise, I did as requested."

"What really happened is they searched his computer, took his hard and jump drives, searched his car, and found pictures of other women as well as several sexual sadist implements."

"Wow. I see why Phillip was so pissed. He'd been exposed for what he is."

"I knew he was trouble, but I had no idea how much. Phillip came home and went after Lisa for a round of his fun and games. Except by that time, I knew everything. My daughter told him to get out. She already had his bags packed.

When he threatened her with the pictures, Lisa told him to go ahead if he could find them."

"He checked his computer, and the hard drive was gone. He flew into a rage and stormed out. Security had his car waiting. I guess he found a place to get drunk and went after Jennifer. If I'd had any idea, I'd have warned her."

Jacks sat forward. "It's like I told the girls, this is no one's fault but Phillip's."

"Right. The other item I wanted to discuss is to offer my hospitality during Jennifer's recovery."

"Okay." Jacks sipped his drink.

"I'd like Jennifer and the girls to stay here after she's discharged, whether Phillip is in custody or not. Lisa would like to be there for all three of them. The girls would have security around the clock. I can provide Dr. Ryan anything she needs."

"Sounds like a plan. We may have to convince Jennifer. She's very independent."

"My thought exactly. Perhaps if we all present a joint campaign..."

"I can go with that. I didn't see Lisa this afternoon. Is she okay?"

"She's doing all right. I think she feels responsible. I know she wanted to give you time with the girls. The guards won't leave their side while you're away."

"Would you please tell her no one is upset with her? Jennifer asked about her while I was visiting. She wanted me to make sure Lisa was okay."

"I'll relay the message. I sent a crime scene clean-up crew to take care of the house and had the locks changed. I hope I didn't overstep. I thought it was important to have it done quickly."

"I hadn't even thought about those things."

"Keep me posted on Jennifer's progress and anything she might need."

The two men stood. "Thank you, Adam. For everything."

They shook hands. "No problem."

Jacks told the girls goodbye and headed back to the hospital. Adam Wallingford would take good care of Jennifer until he returned. That would make heading back to the ship a bit easier when the time came. He pushed the panic of having to leave from his heart. Thinking about right now was what he had to do. The future would take care of itself.

Chapter Twenty

Jacks sat in the window seat of Jennifer's room; he was glad Lisa had remained at the Wallingford estate. Even if he'd played the guilt card of Lisa helping with the girls. The fact Phillip hadn't been arrested had everyone on edge.

He let his thoughts drift. He wanted to hold her. Protect her. But he was afraid he might upset her. She needed to know he was here for the long haul. She was on the road to recovery. Therapy was going well. All he could do was return to the boat and finish the deployment. Hopefully, when he returned, they would begin their lives as a family, if Jennifer would have him.

"Baby, you look so serious. What are you thinking about?" Jennifer asked. She moved slowly and sat on the ottoman.

Jacks checked her face. Most of the swelling was gone. The bruises were fading. "All the progress you've made. I figured you'd be in the hospital longer. I've got to head back in a couple of days."

"When you return, I'll be one hundred percent. Can you hold me for a while?"

"Absolutely." He opened his arms. She slid next to him. He watched her face wince at the pain. She placed her head on his shoulder.

"Sweetheart, I love you. I'm going to miss you," Jennifer whispered.

"I love you, too," Jacks murmured into her hair.

Jennifer shifted several times, let out a sharp breath, and said, "This feels so good. But the position isn't working. Too much pain. Will you take a nap with me? I need to feel you near me."

"Of course."

They settled on the double-size lounge chair, her head on his shoulder. "This is nice. I want to make love to you. But I'm scared," Jennifer whispered, stroking his chest.

"Baby, I know. We can't anyway." Jacks played with the short curls of her new haircut. "The doctor says not for six weeks. We'll cross that bridge when I come home. You're in control. We're taking this relationship at your pace. Please relax. That's all I want. Can you do that for me?"

"What if we can't make love again? What kind of relationship would that be for you?" The tears spilled on his chest.

He kissed her on the top of her head. "Can we worry about that when you're better? I love you. I'll always be here. Okay?"

Jennifer's tears turned to sobs.

Jacks held tight as her body shook. "Baby, it'll be okay." He tried to find the words to reassure her. But none came. To his relief, her crying slowed, and she drifted into sleep.

How could he explain holding her made him feel complete? This was the only place he wanted to be. The last few months of the deployment were going to be hell. He closed his arms tighter around his love and joined her in sleep.

He woke to the sound of the twins talking and

giggling as they approached the room. "Hello, ladies, how was school?" Jacks said when the pair entered the room.

"It was all good. Mom, how are you feeling?" Morgan asked.

"Better now," she said. Jacks could hear the forced lift in her voice.

"Good. You two want to go for pizza for dinner?" Jacks asked.

"That would be great," Morgan said.

"Can Miss Lisa go with us?" Madison asked.

"Sure. Would you ask her and get started on your homework?" Jennifer said.

Morgan paused at the door. "Mr. Jacks, when do you go back to your boat?"

"Day after tomorrow."

"How long will you be gone?"

"About four months."

"We'll keep writing."

"You have no idea how much that helps. I need you to watch after your mother. Make sure she takes it easy."

"We can do that, right, Madison?"

"We certainly can."

****

Jennifer walked down the hall to her room. It would soon be time for her and the girls to go home. But Mr. Wallingford, no, Adam, was probably right. It was better if she stayed at the estate until Phillip was caught. It was very nice here. Lisa went out of her way to make them feel welcome. They'd formed a new family.

Yes. Adam was wonderful with the girls, but he spoiled them rotten. They had teased him earlier that day about picking a grandpa name. He was a great role model for the girls. With Jacks, his family, Adam, and Lisa in their corner, the girls would be fine.

Seconds after turning on the light, the hair on the back of her neck stood up. The warning was too late. She was met with a gun pointed in her direction, and the sight of Lisa's nude bloody body crumpled on the floor.

"Don't say a word, or I'll shoot you right here. Close the door," Phillip said, pointing the gun barrel toward the door.

"What did you do to Lisa?" she asked and started toward her friend.

"Stop right there. As for Lisa, nothing she didn't deserve. Don't worry; she isn't dead yet. Whether she lives or dies is up to you."

"What are you talking about?"

"Undress and do it slowly. I want to enjoy the show. While you do, I'll tell you all."

She looked toward the dresser and saw her emergency alarm. *Damn why had she taken her emergency alarm bracelet off?* "What did I do to make you hate me so much?"

"It isn't what you did. It was what you didn't do."

"What do you mean?"

"You never needed me. You always had all the answers. Even in bed, you took control. You never begged for me to do anything to you. That was until I really hurt you."

"Lisa always asked what she could do. I was nice to her in the beginning. I made her pay every night for getting pregnant. I could get her high, and she would do anything I asked. Especially if I told her it was the last time and I'd never make her do the things she detested again. Lisa went to bed with other men and women for me. Poor thing even had to watch while I made sweet love to other women. She believed I'd stop making her do all the things she hated. Occasionally, I'd be a wonderful, gentle lover, and she was happy.

"Now I'm going to do the same to you. Make love to you one more time. Followed by a repeat performance of the last time we were together. Except this time when I'm done with you, you'll choose who'll die, you or Lisa. Now get undressed. Or do you want me to do it for you? I have my knife right here." He patted his pocket. "You love playing the scared girl like I taught you?"

"Phillip, that was a game we played. You never hurt me," Jennifer stammered and began to slowly unbutton her shirt.

"Slut, this is all your fault, get undressed now." This time he spit the demand and took two steps toward her.

"How did you get in here?"

"Through the garden, I used a small gate when I left and didn't want to be seen. I'm smarter than all of you put together."

If she couldn't talk him down, Jennifer had to stall for time. One of the staff would come looking if she was late for dinner. "Phillip, don't you understand you helped me become the strong assertive woman I am? I was scared to go to college, and you encouraged me. You were the one who got me through my math classes." She inched closer to the dresser and her emergency alarm.

Phillip stared at her with eyes that seemed to be dead inside. Her ex-husband was gone. There was a stranger watching her.

"Don't you remember the night you came home with roses and wine when I graduated? We made love on that old sofa, the one we bought for twenty-five dollars.

I wouldn't have joined the Air Force if you hadn't been there to help me. You pushed me to continue for my master's degree and Ph.D.

"Remember the night I threw my dissertation in the trash and cried? There you were, telling me how smart I was, encouraging me to finish while I was pregnant with the twins. I only wanted to make you proud of me." She saw a brief glimmer in his eyes. For an instant, Jennifer thought she'd made some headway.

"Shut up bitch, and strip."

"Let's go any place you want. Put a blanket over Lisa. I'll go with you. I'll do whatever you ask, I promise. Have I ever lied to you? Even when I knew you didn't want to hear it? Please. We can leave out the back door."

Jennifer prayed she'd reached Phillip.

"Strip, damn you. I want to see the show you've been giving that squid. If Lisa hadn't gone running to you and talked to Mr. Wallingford, none of this would have happened," Phillip yelled, shoving Jennifer against the dresser. "This is a big house. No one can hear you, and if someone does, you'll all die."

She unbuttoned her blouse slowly and dropped it on the floor. "Do you think that's what happened? That wasn't it at all. Our daughters overheard a conversation between you and Lisa. You threatened and then hit Lisa if she didn't do what you told her to. Then they heard what you said about them."

"That's not true."

"You said the only reason you had Morgan and Madison come visit every other weekend was because it pissed me off. Also, how you couldn't care less about the two spoiled brats."

"You're lying. Finish undressing; I never said that."

"Yes, you did, Daddy. I heard you," Madison said. Phillip had been so intent on Jennifer that he hadn't heard the door open.

"I did too, Daddy. Please don't hurt Mommy again!" Morgan yelled as tears ran down her face.

Morgan pushed the button on her bracelet. "Daddy, please don't hurt us anymore. We love you. Even after what you did to Mom, she told us not to blame you. So did Mr. Jacks. We'll leave with you right now if you stop."

Phillip appeared frozen.

Madison spoke again. "Come on, Daddy, Mom won't do anything. Will you, Mom?"

Jennifer caught sight of Charlie outside the door. "Phillip, I won't stop you. The girls want to be with you. Please, if you're going to kill me, get them out of the room. Do not let them see that."

Phillip lowered the gun and walked to the door behind his daughters. When the girls were clear, Charlie and Billy jumped. They caught Phillip off-guard and pushed him to the floor. They struggled, and the gun went off. Jennifer didn't wait to see who was shot. She was at Lisa's side.

She covered her body with the bedspread. "Lisa, are you awake?"

Lisa responded with a murmur.

"Lay still. The ambulance will be here soon. You're going to be okay, I promise. Hang in there."

"Miss Lisa, we're here, too. We love you. Please be okay," Morgan said. Both girls held Lisa's hand.

Lisa was taken to the hospital in a helicopter. Phillip had a gunshot to his shoulder and was taken away in handcuffs.

Jennifer sat on the end of her bed, holding tight to her daughters. "I love you so much. I thought you were going to the movies with your friends?"

"Mr. Wallingford said we could have friends over and watch the movie on the big screen."

"I thought the movie wasn't on video yet."

"It isn't. Lisa's dad said he happened to find a copy."

Chapter Twenty-One

Jennifer, Jacks' parents, Kimberly, and the girls sat at the table in the hangar. Max and Alex flanked Jennifer like fortress walls. The pair had been with her every second of their free time.

The large metal building was decorated with banners, balloons, and signs. Beer, sodas, and champagne were on ice in large wash tubs. A red, white, and blue American flag sheet cake took center stage of a table filled with more food than an army could eat.

The F-18s taxied two by two toward the hangar, moving in tandem, coming to rest facing each other. This continued until twelve planes were in formation. On command, the pilots released the canopies, and all opened like synchronized swimmers.

With the same military accuracy, the crew chiefs set ladders against the jets. The aviators climbed from their cockpits. On the ground, each exchanged a salute for red roses wrapped in navy blue paper tied with white ribbons.

Morgan and Madison ran to meet Jacks. He hugged both girls and presented each with a small bouquet of mixed flowers. The three walked together to Jennifer. Jacks handed her a dozen red roses and said, "Hello, my love, I sure missed you."

"Welcome home. These are beautiful," Jennifer said, smelling the roses. "Thanks for thinking of the girls," she added and stepped into Jacks' arms. She looked into his eyes and asked, "Are you going to kiss me or not?"

That was the invitation he was waiting for. Jacks lifted her chin slightly and kissed her slow and soft. He broke the kiss and whispered, "I love you."

He began to release her, but she held on tight and whispered, "I love you, too. You have no idea how happy I am you're home."

As she loosened her hold, he kissed her again. He released her momentarily to greet his family. After a champagne toast, the pilots reported to turn in their paperwork.

When he returned, the group was enjoying the goodies and visiting with the other families. He walked behind Jennifer and placed his hands on her shoulders. He was the only person that saw her jump at his touch. He leaned in and spoke softly. "Hey, good-looking. What's the plan from here?'

"Your parents parked their motor coach at my house. The girls, your mom, and I cooked several of your favorite foods, and there are also steaks in the refrigerator."

"Any chance you made blueberry muffins?"

"I have everything to bake them for breakfast tomorrow. The girls baked chocolate chip cookies this morning. Shall we head out?"

"Sounds like a plan," Jacks said, taking Jennifer's hand. He was ready to settle in and see what the future would hold for them. He fought back the panicked thoughts that Phillip might have ruined everything. No. He'd not give him that power over their lives.

****

"Henry, would you and Martha like something to drink?" Jennifer asked.

"Yes, coffee would be wonderful," Henry said.

"For me as well," Martha added.

"I can fix it, Mom," Morgan said.

"Mr. and Mrs. Williams, would you like some cookies? We baked them this morning," Madison asked.

"Sounds lovely, thanks," Martha said.

"Jacks, your things are in the spare room. I'll get you towels so you can take a nice, long, hot shower."

Jacks said, "That sounds wonderful. Girls, I'll have some of those cookies and a glass of very cold milk when I'm done. Your chocolate chip cookies were the hit of the squadron."

"Let us know when you're ready," Morgan said.

"You got it."

Jennifer headed upstairs toward the spare room. When she and Jacks were alone, he turned to face her. "Sweetie, how are you really doing?"

"I'm okay. I've been working with a counselor and have made great progress. Occasionally, I get caught off guard. I'm glad you're here. I love how it feels being in your arms. I know you want to make love—"

Jacks placed his fingertips on her lips. "Baby, we'll take all the time you need. I'm not going anywhere. We'll take one day at a time. Your schedule. Can I hold you?"

"Please, yes."

He held her and let her cry. "Darling, it'll be okay, I promise. I love you."

She stepped back and handed him towels, and led him down the hall to her bedroom. "Use my bathroom and take all the time you need. Shower or soak in the tub.

I guess you remember the tub has great jets."

"Any chance you'd like to take a soak with me later tonight? I can wash your back. But only if you're okay with it?" he quickly added. "Sorry, should I be asking you things like this?"

She slid her arms around his neck and said, "Darling, please ask or say anything that's on your mind. Same goes for touching me. Go with what you feel. I'll let you know if it makes me uncomfortable. Like this afternoon when you touched me and I jumped, you didn't pull away. That's what I need. I'd love to take a bath with you once everyone is in bed. Your clothes aren't in the spare room. They're in the same place as before in my room. I love you." She kissed him quickly and started toward the door.

Before she could make it into the hall, he spoke, "Sweetheart."

"Yes," Jennifer said, and she turned to see Jacks holding out his hand.

"Can you come back for a minute?"

She stepped back into the room.

"I'd love to have a kiss. One small one would do."

She turned the simple kiss into one that set his senses spinning out of control. Jacks ran his hands through Jennifer's short hair and met her passion with his own.

When the kiss ended, she said, "Oh, my God, sweetie, it feels so good."

"I know, darling. You better leave now, or we may find ourselves in your bed. I think you might be missed if that happens."

"See you in a bit," Jennifer said as a smile crossed her face.

Jacks stood under the hot stream of water until it turned cold.

He headed toward the kitchen but found it empty. The sight outside the large picture window made him smile. His parents were sitting on the wooden glider. Jennifer was on the swing. The three were watching Madison and Morgan playing fetch with the herd of dachshunds. With his parent's dogs, the count was five. The sight of the two families intermingled overwhelmed him.

****

Jacks smiled at the pile of sleeping dogs. They'd played themselves out. He checked on the girls. It appeared he and Jennifer were alone. He found her on the porch swing. "May I join you?"

"Sure."

He held her hand and enjoyed the evening breeze. Both were quiet for a long time.

"Baby, you tired?" Jennifer asked, breaking the silence.

"A bit. It's been a long day."

"Would you like to head to bed?" she asked.

"Sure, in a bit. There's something I'd like to talk about."

He stood and got down on one knee and looked up. "Baby, will you marry me?"

"Oh, Jacks, I want nothing more, but I need time. I'm not sure I can be a wife in the way you need. What if we can never make love? What if I can't give you children? You have to think all those things through."

"I have. Tell me what you would tell a client who was going through the same experience. Recommend that they give up or hide in a shell someplace? Never think about loving someone again? What if I had come back to you missing a limb or couldn't take you to bed and please you like before? Would you toss me aside? Why give Phillip that kind of power?"

"It's not the same."

"Well, explain that to me, Madam Doctor. What's the difference?" When she said nothing, he continued, "Okay, now your second argument about children. In my eyes, I already have two. If there are more children, wonderful. If not, one day, I hope to be there when the twins graduate, get married, and make us old, gray grandparents."

"I'm not sure," Jennifer said.

He stood and reached out his hand. "Come with me. We'll just hold each other close tonight."

"Okay."

Jacks could see the apprehension in her face, "Come on, beautiful. We can even keep our clothes on."

Jacks led her into the house. Jennifer locked the door, turned on the alarm, and headed toward the bedroom. They cuddled on the bed and drifted off to sleep. Several hours later, Jacks was awakened to Jennifer pushing to move away from him. Quickly the whimpers turned into cries. "Baby, it's Jacks. I'm right here."

She opened her eyes, crawled back into his arms, and let the tears out. He held her close and said nothing.

"Jacks, I'm sorry."

"About what? You had a nightmare. How often do they happen?"

"Every few nights, I guess. It depends on my level of stress."

"I'll go to the other room so you can sleep."

"No, please stay."

He pulled her close again, kissed her forehead, and they fell into a deep sleep.

****

The next morning, Jennifer awoke alone. Panic set in. Had Jacks left during the night? Then she saw the note and the rose.

Darling, I hope you're able to sleep late. The girls, my parents, and I are dropping the dogs at the groomer, taking the girls to the library, and to get a smoothie. If we're not back when you're up and around, give me a call. The girls set the security alarm. Oh, and I love you!

She glanced at the clock. It was one in the afternoon. She hadn't slept that late since the attack. As she was climbing out of bed, she heard her daughters' laughter. Jacks slowly opened the door and peered inside. "Look, she's up."

"Mommy," the girls chimed in together. They jumped on the bed and hugged her. "We had so much fun. We dropped the dogs at the groomer. Mr. Jacks let us drive his car. It was awesome."

"He did? Well, well." Jennifer shifted her eyes to Jacks and smiled.

"We picked out clothes for all the dogs. Halloween costumes, collars, Christmas dresses for the girls, bows, and matching ankle bracelets."

"That's wonderful. Sounds like you had quite a day."

"We did and got seafood for dinner. Jacks' parents are going to cook on the grill. We have shrimp, lobster, scallops, and oysters still in the shell. I promised to try a grilled oyster. Mr. Brandon and Ms. Kimberly are coming over."

"It sounds like we're going to have a big night."

"Mom, will you make cheese grits?" Madison asked.

"Sure."

"And hush puppies?" Morgan added.

"No problem."

"I do have one question. Did anyone think to bring me a smoothie?"

"We sure did," Jacks said as he handed her the cup he'd been hiding behind his back.

"Thanks for taking the girls out, I'm going to get up, get in the shower, and I'll join you in the kitchen."

"Okay." With that, the girls were off.

"Sometimes they're all grown up, and others they're little girls again. I remember that age—from day to day, your mood changes."

"Baby, they're wonderful young ladies. Mom and Dad are very impressed by their manners, intelligence, and sense of humor."

"Thanks."

"I'll be in the kitchen," Jacks said as he headed toward the bedroom door.

"Jacks, there's something I want you to see. You must be completely honest with your answer. Promise?"

****

"Okay." Jacks felt like he was walking into an enemy trap. He had no idea what was coming.

She slipped out of her shirt and sweatpants. As she turned, he saw there were scars where there had once been smooth skin.

"So, what do you think? And please tell me the truth."

"First of all, I always tell you the truth. I've done

that from the start, right?"

"Yes," she said nodding her head.

He walked to the bathroom, removed her robe from the back of the door, and returned to her. "Please put this on. I can't have this conversation with you nude."

After she put on the robe, she stared at the floor.

Jacks placed his hand on her chin and slowly lifted it until their eyes met. "Jennifer, I can't talk to you without clothes on because all I want to do is touch you. Kiss all the places that make you tremble for me. Watch your eyes glaze over when you give yourself to me completely. Not to be crude, but you asked for honesty. Look at my jeans, and you'll see how I react to your body. I'm as hard as a rock with one glance. Hell, I react that way every time you step into my arms."

"But what if —"

He reached out and placed one finger on her lips. "What ifs are gone, my love. You're stuck with me unless you tell me to leave. I'm going to be right here with this ring burning a hole in my pocket." He patted his hand on his jacket pocket, "until you decide to marry me. No matter how long it takes. So, get dressed and come join the fun." He kissed her on the forehead. Before he opened the door, he said, "By the way, when was the last time you slept this late?"

"Not for a long time. I guess at the mountains or at the beach, only when we're together."

"Well, beautiful, I'm the only common dominator. Take that into consideration. If nothing else, you'll sleep better with me around." Jacks winked, opened the door, left the room, and quietly closed the door behind him.

****

Jennifer's mood took a sharp upward turn. She

showered, dressed, and headed into the kitchen full of positive spirits. It would be okay. Jacks loved her. She loved him so very much. They would work this out together. He was right. She'd marry him, and they'd be a family. The future would be what they made it. Everything seemed perfect when she entered the kitchen. Her daughters were there getting treats for the dogs.

"Mom, we're going into the backyard to play with the dogs," Morgan said.

"I'll get some juice and be right with you." As she placed the juice back in the refrigerator, there was a knock at the front door. She walked to the door and looked through the peephole. There were Brandon and Kimberly.

Jennifer's reaction caught her by surprise. Her heart began to pound. Beads of sweat rolled down her back. She fought to catch her breath. "Breathe," she told herself. It was a full-blown panic attack. In seconds, all the memories and emotions of the attack flooded in. She managed to take a deep breath and opened the door.

"Greetings," Brandon said as he hugged Jennifer.

She felt the color drain from her face.

Kimberly hugged her friend and asked, "Where's everyone?"

"Out back," Jennifer said, fighting to keep her voice steady.

"Brandon, grab yourself a beer and head on out. We'll be there in a minute." Kimberly said.

"Okay, ladies."

When he was gone, Kimberly led Jennifer to the sofa. "What's going on? You look like you saw a ghost."

Jennifer lowered her head and spoke with tears. "I was fine. I looked out the peephole and saw you two. All the fear and helplessness I felt the night of the attack hit me full force." Jennifer felt her positive mood drain from her body. "Jacks wants me to marry him. How can I do that? Tie him to a woman who can't even answer the door without falling apart?"

"Sweetie, do you love him?"

"Yes."

"Do you want to be with him?"

"Yes."

"You know he understands the situation?"

"Yes."

"Then what's the problem?"

Her words poured out like water from a pitcher. "He has to want children. What if I can't give him that? What if we can never make love? What if he's only asking me because he feels guilty?"

"I hate to rain on your pity parade, but Jacks had the ring long before the attack. He was going to ask you to marry him in Spain. He had it all worked out, including talking to the girls before he popped the question. In case you missed it, the man's head-over-heels in love with you. He'll work through this with you."

A ray of hope began to shine within Jennifer. "Are you sure?"

"Jennifer, as your friend, I'll kick your butt if you don't say yes and soon."

"Thanks."

"Don't sound so enthused. What did the doctor say at your check-up?"

"I'm progressing well. The medical board is going to force me to retire because of the injuries to my back. The official word hasn't come down yet. But I have friends passing me information. The truth is I can't be deployed into a war zone due to my injuries. Plus, I've been diagnosed with PTSD. Basically, the medical board thinks I'll freak out under stress. I'm going to be given full retirement with one hundred percent disability."

"Wow, what did Jacks say?" When she didn't answer, Kimberly continued, "Let me guess. You haven't told him?"

"I'm waiting for the documentation. All of this has taken so much from me."

"Stop it now. Take back your life and what you want. I know this is cliché. What if the situation were reversed? Jacks was injured and unable to make love with you, have children, and was forced to retire. Would you walk away from him?"

"Of course not, but this is different."

"How?"

"That would be out of his control. I'm a psychologist with years of training. I should've seen how Phillip's mental health was deteriorating. Jacks tried to tell me, but I didn't listen, and look what happened."

"You're so full of shit. What would you tell a client in this situation?"

"Where's my beautiful woman," Jacks said as he walked through the house.

"We're in here," Kimberly said. "I needed a bit of counseling, and Jennifer said she would squeeze me in."

"Can you squeeze me in, my love?" His smile touched her heart.

Kimberly spoke as she stood. She patted Jacks on the shoulder. "Please, young love makes me sick. I need a beer and my husband."

When she was gone, Jacks looked down into Jennifer's eyes, "Would you do me a favor?"

"What?"

"Would you make the cheese grits with extra sharp cheddar cheese?"

She sat back on the sofa and laughed.

"What's so funny?" Jacks asked, raising an eyebrow.

"Nothing. That's the last thing I expected you to ask."

"I could lie and say I wanted to see if you were okay. Or that I was curious to see what you two were up to. But I want to be with you."

She patted the sofa beside her. "Sit, please. I had a panic attack when I looked through the peephole. Kimberly was reading me the riot act about my stupid excuses for not marrying you. And finally, I'm going to be forced to retire from the Air Force."

"So, the upside is you're getting better, everyone except you realizes you should marry me, and you'll be free to travel with me and practice when you like. Or stay home with our children. And before you object to the children, I'm referring to the two young ladies who have my father, a very serious Navy Admiral, acting in a very unmilitary manner. Do I have all the bases covered?"

"I guess you do. I love you, and yes, I'll marry you."

"Wait, I'm not down on one knee." Jacks knelt in front of Jennifer and asked again, "Jennifer, will you marry me?"

"Yes!"

He reached in his pocket, removed the ring, and slipped it on her finger.

A word about the author...

EJ Towler lives in coastal Virginia and writes tales of extraordinary women and the men they love (or sometimes simply tolerate). Writing about military heroes, heroines, and villains comes naturally as she served in the United States Army. She currently has two published novels, Stealth Maneuvers, and One Little Lie. EJ's stories have unusual twists and turns, but none begin on a dark and stormy night. Her books feature dachshunds who find their forever homes. She and her dachshund medical alert/service dog, Huckleberry Hound, travel for research, book signings, and fun.

http://ejtowler.com
@Towlerej
@Huckdachshundservicedog
@Huckservicedog

Thank you for purchasing
this publication of The Wild Rose Press, Inc.

For questions or more information
contact us at
info@thewildrosepress.com.

The Wild Rose Press, Inc.
www.thewildrosepress.com